T0147927

THE MYSTERY OF THE TIMEHRI ROCK PAINTINGS

THE MYSTERY OF THE TIMEHRI ROCK PAINTINGS

Claurence D. C. Johnson

iUniverse LLC
Bloomington

THE MYSTERY OF THE TIMEHRI ROCK PAINTINGS

Copyright © 2013 by Claurence D. C. Johnson.

All rights reserved. *No part of this book may be used or reproduced by any means, graphic, electronic, or mechanical, including photocopying, recording, taping or by any information storage retrieval system without the written permission of the publisher except in the case of brief quotations embodied in critical articles and reviews.*

This is a work of fiction. All of the characters, names, incidents, organizations, and dialogue in this novel are either the products of the author's imagination or are used fictitiously.

iUniverse books may be ordered through booksellers or by contacting:

iUniverse LLC
1663 Liberty Drive
Bloomington, IN 47403
www.iuniverse.com
1-800-Authors (1-800-288-4677)

Because of the dynamic nature of the Internet, any web addresses or links contained in this book may have changed since publication and may no longer be valid. The views expressed in this work are solely those of the author and do not necessarily reflect the views of the publisher, and the publisher hereby disclaims any responsibility for them.

Any people depicted in stock imagery provided by Thinkstock are models, and such images are being used for illustrative purposes only.
Certain stock imagery © Thinkstock.

ISBN: 978-1-4759-9967-9 (sc)
ISBN: 978-1-4759-9968-6 (ebk)

Library of Congress Control Number: 2013913008

Printed in the United States of America

iUniverse rev. date: 08/07/2013

CONTENTS

Chapter

1. Mysterious Symbols 1
2. A stolen letter 8
3. A helpful Mr. Sam 17
4. A narrow escape 24
5. The night prowler 29
6. Eddie tapes a message 36
7. An elusive suspect 43
8. Meeting Supt. Clarke 49
9. Eddie is captured 55
10. The message is deciphered 61
11. Trailing a suspect 70
12. Saving Eddie 80
13. The capture of Alfie walcott 92
14. The hidden bomb 109
15. Henry disappears 121
16. The mystery unfolds 130
17. Trapped in a cave 140
18. The gang is rescued 148

I thank all those loving persons who helped me complete this book. I am grateful to all the tutors and staff of Cyril Potter College of Education and especially the entire student body of the 1974-1977 graduating class.

Thanks to John Rawlins and Rocksandy Jordan and the boys of the dormitory, you will always be remembered.

Finally, I wish to dedicate this book to all the boys and girls of Guyana.

CDC Johnson (April, 1975)

Mysterious Symbols

I t was a cool sunny day in the warm town of Turkeyen. *A typical day*, James thought as he climbed the stairs with his best friends Eddie and Henry. They always heard the sounds of birds in Guyana, and the Teachers Training College Campus was no different. A light breeze from the Atlantic Ocean was always a delight on hot days.

'When are we going to have lunch?' asked Eddie. He was about to walk up the stairs backwards. His friends always marveled at that skill but they waited for him to trip one day.

'Well I would love to have pepper pot,' laughed Henry, knowing that was Eddie's favourite dish. 'And isn't it too early to be thinking of lunch,' he said smiling.

James was anxious to finally get school over with, since he was eager to teach the next generation the struggles of Guyana. He knew that a new country would only be prosperous with a well-taught next generation. This was 1976 and he was glad Guyana was finally an independent nation ready to plot its own course, but he knew it had a long way to go.

This was usually James' thought most mornings as he walked into class for their history lesson. James knew that he and his friends had the habit of being the first ones into class. 'Hey fellas, I'm off to the bathroom. Don't get into mischief,' he said smiling, knowing his friends loved to pull pranks on him.

'Sure!' they shouted after him in a laughing manner.

'Tuesday, Tuesday,' said Eddie, as he pulled his chair from under the fashionable table he occupied in the education room.

'Is Tuesday your unlucky day, Eddie?' Henry asked, also taking a comfortable seat at the adjoining table sitting crossed legged and surveying Eddie.

'No, not at all, it's not the day I don't like, it is the subject that we do on this day!'

Henry sat straight up and surveyed his friend. Henry noticed that he was not as tall and compact as himself. Eddie was medium height and of Amerindian descent. He had often encouraged Eddie to join him at the gym but to little success.

Feeling the stuffiness of the room, Henry soon rose to his feet, walked across to the closed window to let a light breeze blow through. The humidity was always an issue during the summer, a thing Guyanese were accustomed to, but at times felt it unbearable. Henry reached the window and gave it a tug since it was difficult to pry open.

'Dive, look out!'

Hearing this warning and moving purely on instinct, Henry dived head first, exhibiting all the skills that he accumulated as one of the college's best goalkeepers. Just as Henry touched the well-polished wooden floor, a huge glass shade from the light fixture crashed mere inches away, splattering broken glass.

Henry lay prostrate and half dazed. Was he dreaming or had he just missed being seriously injured?

Eddie reached his friend slowly getting him up. 'Are you hurt?' he asked, bending over and extracting a piece of glass from Henry's crop of woolly hair.

'No, I don't think so. I heard a faint squeak and looked up, and saw the over-hanging fluorescent light metal casing move slightly and heard your shouts,' he exhaled feeling slightly shaken up.

'Oh brother, that was a close call!'

'This fallen shade must have sounded throughout the building. Look, all the students are hurrying to the scene of the miniature explosion,' laughed Henry.

'What happened?' asked James running into the classroom.

'I don't know,' Henry told him, 'I was just opening the window when Eddie shouted to dive. It's a lucky thing that I did or I would have been seriously hurt,' he added, pointing to the mass of broken glass littering the unusually glittering floor.

Just then there was a voice from the rear of the mass of students, who were now starting to gather outside the classroom. 'Any cuts or bruises?' asked the deep voice which was dwarfing the questions posed by enquiring students.

'No, Mr. Simon,' Henry answered, 'only a few bruises on my elbows and a dirty shirt. It's a pity that we have to wear white shirts to classes.'

'Well, we can attend to your bruises, but there is nothing that can be done about the white shirt. It's part of the College's uniform and more than that, we have to adhere to the rules of the institution at all times,' Mr. Simon the resident tutor, said emphatically.

'So what can I do?' he asked looking pensive.

'You'll have to change of course, but first, visit Nurse Kaladeen to have your bruises checked and possibly bandaged.'

'Mr. Simon, all my uniforms are in the laundry, my shirts I mean,' said Henry.

'You have a problem indeed. Under these current circumstances I will allow you to wear something else. Remember, nothing brightly colored.' he said using his customary finger wagging he gave all students.

'Thank you Mr. Simon, I'll do my best not to get into Miss Triumph's way. I know how strict she is about the dress code.' Henry thought Mrs. Triumph's strictness for the dress code was too old fashioned and circumspect, an opinion he usually voiced to Mr. Simon but chose not to at this serious moment.

'Alright boys, precious time is being wasted, he said quickly glancing at his broad wristwatch. 'It is after nine o'clock and you are students that should be in your classrooms.'

'We'll get the room cleaned,' James said, as Mr. Simon turned and headed towards the tutorial quarters signaling the matter was closed.

All the inquisitive students who had gathered at the scene of the accident took their cue from Mr. Simon and started trickling to their various lecture rooms.

'I wonder how this shade fell from its hooks. After all, these things are supposed to be very strong,' James wondered loudly.

Eddie and Henry nodded as they observed the glass splattered room with their friend.

'Probably the result of careless workmanship, or the hooks became weak due to constant pressure,' suggested Eddie.

'I don't think that constant pressure caused it, after all there are larger shades in the multi-purpose hall. Also, this building is practically new,' said James.

'That may be so, but,' began Eddie, before he was interrupted by Henry.

'But nothing,' Henry interrupted, 'the fact remains that I was almost seriously injured by this shade that accidentally fell from its hooks.'

'Accidentally. I wonder if someone had deliberately tampered with this shade. Maybe they were hiding something in the ceiling and had to leave quickly.'

'What a notion! I just don't see any sense in that at all,' said Eddie, 'Tampering with college property! Who would do that?'

'Exactly! However we teenagers away from home usually engage in many pranks,' said James, eyeing his friends.

Indeed, college days were full of fun and the pranks that were perpetrated were incredible, James thought. A few nights before, there was a dormitory fight between the middle and the lower floor. He knew Franklin and his group had used the fire hoses to drench the rooms on the middle floor and the boys on the lower floor retaliated with the fire hoses at full blast. After an hour, their battle grounds were inundated with water and beds were practically afloat.

'Why make such a fuss over frivolous things?' asked Henry. 'No damage has been done and after a visit to Nurse Kaladeen she will have me patched up in no time,' he said with a smile.

Nurse Omadevi Kaladeen was the college's resident nurse and her tenderness and loving care often proved to be more effective than the medications she administered. Every male student loved the prospect of visiting Nurse Kaladeen. She was young and attractive, with long black hair and an enchanting smile. Girls also loved visiting her because she understood their anxieties and was always willing to recommend a day's bed rest.

'Oh Nurse Kaladeen.' Eddie said in a dreamy voice. 'She apparently loves her job, having to put up with all three hundred and sixty young adults like us.'

'Solving this mystery I guess will have to wait,' James said. 'A piece of state property has been destroyed. I think it should be up to us to at least supply some good reasons why.'

His friends knew James was an amateur detective and usually took control of these situations. Both Eddie and Henry smiled over James' head as they could tell he was anxious to use his detective skills. Henry knew his friend had briefly thought of entering the police force and being a detective as his uncle was.

'Okay, where do we start then, what should we do, what clues do we have?' Eddie asked James looking for direction.

'We can start by cleaning up this mess, then climbing up to the ceiling to inspect whether the shade fell on its own.' As James spoke his he bent down and picked up a piece of crumpled paper from the broken glass.

'Why bother with a piece of paper, why pick it up?' asked Eddie, 'We could just sweep all of it into the trash container.'

'I don't like seeing paper on the floor, it looks rather awful,' James answered with a shrug of his broad shoulders. He instinctively began to smooth out the paper taking care not to get pieces of glass on his hands.

James began surveying the piece of paper intently. 'What is it James?' Henry asked, noticing a confused look on his face.

'Just a few scribbles,' he said turning the paper from side to side. 'Something about these drawings looks familiar. I think that I have seen these patterns somewhere before.' He then turned the off-white paper to his friends.

Henry edged closer to James and looked at the paper. 'Looks like a child's first attempts at drawing and writing to me,' he said lifting his shoulder. 'Maybe one of the modules had preschool role play for psychology class.'

Eddie peered over at the paper in Henry's hand. 'I know these drawings!' he gasped. 'I am an Amerindian and would recognize these anywhere. These are representations of old Amerindian rock paintings, hieroglyphics or petroglyphs.' he added with an air of authority and certainty.

'That's it, I know that they were familiar, I saw them at the National Museum,' chimed James. 'I believe that they are called petroglyphs! The museum's collection is referred to as The Timehri Rock Paintings.'

'Very interesting!' said Henry, 'who would or could have dropped this here? It seems that we have a mystery brewing, fellas,' said James putting the piece of paper carefully into his pocket, then proceeding to put his hand on his chin and pulling the three strands of beard that had announced to the world that he was becoming a full-fledged young adult.

'James, do you think that someone could have deliberately tampered with the shade?' asked Eddie.

'I don't know, but that is what we will hope to find out,' replied James thoughtfully as he adjusted the collar of his shirt and looked pensive as he caressed strands of his beard.

Henry, grabbing a table, moved it under the exposed fluorescent tube and proceeded to climb, being mindful of his feet not being close to the edge of the table.

'See anything?' James asked.

Henry did not answer. He stared at the wires then let out a sharp whistle. 'James, get up here and take a look at this,' he suddenly shouted.

'You have to get off the table first,' James cautioned then laughed. 'It's too small for both of us to stand on.'

Henry eased himself down carefully, avoiding the glass still splattered around the classroom. James took Henry's place on the table and examined the wires that held the heavy shade in place. 'What!' he exclaimed, 'Can it be possible, no it is incredible!'

'Take a look Eddie,' Henry said as James climbed down.

Eddie, not as tall as his friends, took a while longer to hoist himself on the table. When he got up, he meticulously examined the wires and where the shade had been. He nodded his head then heaved himself off the table exhibiting great nimbleness as he landed between two large fragments of glass.

After all three boys had been able to observe, Eddie asked, 'What do you think, James?'

'I think that this wire was deliberately cut,' James said. 'This does not appear to be an accident.'

'Exactly,' added Henry. 'I am getting a strange feeling about this.'

'Who could be so silly to do something so dangerous?' said Eddie.

'A practical joker,' suggested Henry jovially.

'It's not that funny. It may appear that way, but this can be considered sabotage,' said James.

'Any reason why?' asked Eddie.

'I don't know that answer, but with the help of you two we may be able to get some answers and solve this mystery.'

A STOLEN LETTER

'Sounds good to me,' echoed Henry, 'However let's first get your injured friend to see Nurse Kaladeen, as Mr. Simon suggested and get a change of clothes,' he said smiling.

'Don't forget, you already had two sick days for the term, so don't talk her into giving you anymore. Final examinations are a few weeks away and the tutors have begun giving hints of possible examination questions.'

'That's right!' said Eddie 'and we had better sweep this mess up and hurry over to Miss Dorsett's Methodology class.'

Just as they were about to gather the broken glass into a heap, the janitor Mr. Terry hurried in and told them that Mr. Simon had sent him to clean up. Mr. Terry was an affable middle-aged man who seemed to enjoy his job immensely, since he was always whistling softly while he worked. Friday afternoon was his best time since he stopped working early and headed straight to Shaboo's village bar as he said, 'to recharge his batteries for the new week.'

The boys thanked Mr. Terry and with the crumpled piece of paper securely in James' pocket they headed to their first class of the day, and as they later learned from Miss Dorsett, 40 minutes late. After listening to their explanations she was kind enough to let them stand at the back of the classroom and reminded them that as far as she was concerned only sickness or death are valid reasons for students living on a college campus to be late for classes. 'You students believe that you own this campus,' she ended as she motioned them to the back amidst giggles from some of the girls.

After classes were finished for the day James, Eddie and Henry went to their rooms to contemplate the fallen shade, cut wires and the mystery of the petroglyphs. Thinking about how they would set about finding and possibly apprehending the perpetrator or perpetrators was going to be difficult because of such few clues.

The boy's college seemed like an unlikely place for a mystery. They attended Cyril Potter College of Education, which was situated at Turkeyen, five kilometers east of the Garden City of Georgetown. Most students loved the school. The college provided residential facilities for the young teacher trainees who were selected from the three counties of Essequibo, Demerara and Berbice.

The college was constructed of indigenous materials, marking the turning point in building construction and technological achievement in Guyana.

James stared out his window aware that his future alma mater was joined by the long line of established picturesque structures that littered the Georgetown landscape. There were the Law Courts, The Town Hall, and the St. George's Cathedral, the tallest wooden building in the world, the crowning glory of the Garden City of Georgetown.

James heard Henry's casual drumming of his fingers on the table which broke his train of thought about his outdoor surroundings.

'Do you think that the paper with the petroglyphs could have been in the electrical shade?' James asked,

'Why do you ask? It is possible that someone may have hidden it there,' Eddie said.

'A bit absurd if you ask me, but quite possible,' chimed Henry in his usual abrupt manner.

James knew his friends had gotten to understand each other quite well and knew that Eddie was very frugal in the use of words and often tried to avoid lengthy conversations. James sat on his bed in the room he shared with Henry. He thought it was funny that everyone thought they were twins due to them being inseparable from the day that they met at orientation.

'The library is just next door, and they could have hidden it there and have gone to check up some information in a few books,' James reasoned.

'I think so too. We were the first to enter that classroom this morning and I don't remember seeing anything on the floor, but then it could have been an oversight,' Henry concluded.

'Henry, can you remember seeing anything on the floor when you went in?' James asked.

'I am absolutely sure there was nothing there,' he assured him, 'if there was, I would have picked it up.'

'Seems that we are agreed then that the crumpled paper most likely fell with the shade,' James said.

'We should therefore begin our investigating by questioning the cleaners,' Eddie suggested, 'They are the ones who open the classrooms in the mornings.'

'That's a good idea. They can tell us if they saw anything suspicious when they entered the room this morning,' James said.

'How do we to know that this was done this morning?' asked Henry.

'No one is saying that this was done this morning, it could have been yesterday afternoon, or even last night,' said James.

'What proof is there to suggest that, or for you to assume that the wires were cut deliberately as you suggested earlier?' asked Henry.

'First, the cut wire appears to have been done recently,' said James. 'An electrician would have used electrical tape on any such exposed wire long ago.'

James noticed both Eddie and Henry looking at him with skepticism.

'How is it that you take so much interest in the minute details?' asked Henry.

James did not answer, staring blankly at the top of the table and then rested a hand on his chin with his index finger pointing towards his right eye. That meant that he was deep in thought and was getting one of his much vaunted inspirations.

James' father had died in a car accident three years ago when he was fifteen and his grief-stricken mother followed shortly after. He was virtually alone in the world with only his uncle Patrick 'Skip'

Clarke, a detective superintendent, and a cousin, Abiola, who was also a student at the college.

James had aspirations of becoming a private detective but had to forgo those plans when his mother died. He had a love for solving mysteries and as a child read the adventures of Sherlock Holmes and some writings from Agatha Christie. James often wondered why no Caribbean writer had ever attempted a mystery novel. He knew of the numerous world famous Caribbean writers and poets like Edgar Mittleholzer, A. J. Seymour, V. S. Naipaul and Derek Walcott. He often hoped to be the first in a long line to introduce mystery stories based on Guyana to Guyanese and the Caribbean.

Here he was confronted by a mystery and he was determined to solve it. James stood up and walked to the door slowly. 'We should visit the principal and discuss this matter with him. I am sure that he would have gotten a written report from the Mr. Simon by now,' said James.

'Yes, we should do that,' agreed Eddie.

'Okay let's go, squad!' said Henry.

The boys clutched their note pads and text books in their hands and left for the Principal's office.

Mr. Sam had assisted the boys on numerous occasions. He was an amiable man, slightly bald, and probably in his late fifties. The most curious things about him were his agility and the neatly trimmed white beard that he was constantly stroking. He was of mixed Indian and African parentage.

Henry once asked him what inspired him to become a teacher and an educator and he told him that his father was a cane cutter working on the Albion sugar estates. Mr. Sam recalled that, 'Those days were very difficult. My father returned home every night and complained about the sweltering sun and the hard work of filling two or three punts with cut cane every day.'

Henry clearly remembered this conversation as well as the many others he had with the principal and his friends. He and his friends felt a connection with Mr. Sam. Henry felt a stronger connection because he mentioned to Mr. Sam that his grandfather was also a cane cutter, but had worked at Enmore.

Mr. Sam would always mention that cane cutting was 'a lot of back breaking work and no money to show for it.' He always mentioned that his father drilled it into him and his brothers and sisters to get an education and to be somebody in life. With this advice, Mr. Sam won a scholarship and studied in England.

Mr. Sam's secretary was very pleasant and charming and she always smelled the sweetest of fragrances. She waved to the group in greeting and added a wide grin that showed her remarkably white teeth.

'What can I do for you young men today?' she asked in a markedly Buxtonian accent.

'We'd like to speak with Mr. Sam for a few moments, Miss Abrams,' said James.

'You are in luck! He was preparing to leave for a meeting at the university campus. Let me see if he will see you,' she said cheerily.

She got up from her typewriter and told them to sit while she informed the principal that they wanted to have a word with him. The boys sat calmly. Miss Abrams returned and motioned them towards Mr. Sam's door which she had left ajar.

'The principal will see you,' she announced.

'Thank you very much,' they said in unison and with James leading the way they headed for Mr. Sam's office.

Henry knocked on the thick dark wooden door of the Principal's office.

'Come on in,' said the deep bass of Mr. Sam. Henry swung the door open to see the principal leaning forward in his iconic black and gold office chair. Mr. Sam had a forlorn gaze then looked off in the distance out of his office. Henry sensed conviction in the principal's eyes

'Hello boys,' said Mr. Sam.

'Hello Mr. Sam,' the boys said.

'Remember I told you about my younger years,' he said still looking out the window, as the boys slowly nodded in agreement. 'All three of you remind me of myself. The most difficult time I had was eating roti and curried potato three times a day every day. The only time we had meat was on weekends when Pa would pack his fishing net before we woke up and went fishing at big pond,' he said now staring at the boys.

Henry could clearly tell this was Mr. Sam recalling his childhood and finishing the previous conversation the boys had with him.

The principal settled back comfortably in his chair, the boys gave him an account of what had transpired earlier in the morning. He acknowledged that he had received a written report from Mr. Simon, and was thankful that the boys had thought of coming to him.

Mr. Sam got up from his cushioned chair and patted each one of the boys on his shoulder. 'So, my dear young students, get as much education as you can and the world is there for you to conquer. Now off you go, or is there a break period now?' he asked.

The boys discussed later that they got the impression that Mr. Sam, at that moment just wanted to be left alone with memories of his underprivileged childhood and to savour his accomplishments as the principal of the foremost teacher education college in the entire Caribbean.

Heading to their next class, the boys descended the winding stairway, hurried past the science laboratories and finally on to the lush green lawns. Shelly Fraser, a special friend of James, was just entering the Design and Technology Department when she saw them and stopped.

'Hi there!' she called out to them, winking at James. 'Where are you hurrying to?' she asked.

'We are going to the administration office,' Eddie told her.

'For what! At this time of day, you should be doing some extra studies, don't you think?' she scolded affectionately.

'Hello, Shelly,' James said as he gave her a slight embrace. 'It is important,' he informed her.

'I see you are asking for a long vacation to get away from us, is that it?' she teased.

'Now my dear Shelly, don't be ridiculous. Why should I want to get away from the most precious person in my life?' James teased back.

'Please don't flatter me.' Shelly was beginning to blush, smiling and showing her dimples.

'It's not flattery,' Henry said, 'you girls are our souls, and what good is a man without a soul?' he added philosophically.

'Okay you win,' she admitted, 'but tell me why it's so important that you go now?'

'Take a good look at Henry,' advised Eddie pointing at Henry who at the moment just looked tired from climbing the stairway.

She looked at him closely for the first time and saw that his hand was bandaged. She clearly had not heard about what had transpired earlier that morning.

'Henry you are injured!' she exclaimed, 'Did you fall? Did you have an accident?' she asked alarmingly.

She bent down and looked at the bandages that Nurse Kaladeen had put on.

'It's nothing to worry about; I only got just a few bruises. It looks worse than it actually is.'

James then told her briefly what had happened that morning and reassured her that it was just a minor accident.

'Okay if you say so, but I must let Abi and Anita know about this. I am sure that they know nothing or they would have mentioned it to me,' she began to shout as she quickly walked away.

'Bye Shelly! See you later,' the boys chorused.

'You had better be careful,' she cautioned, 'I'm glad that it's nothing serious.'

'James,' Shelly called after them, 'I forgot to tell you, there is a letter for you in the office. I am not sure but I think there is one for Henry also.'

'Thank you, Shelly,' James said as they turned and headed towards the office.

'I wonder who wrote this time?' said Henry with a smile. 'Both Jackie and Yvette owe me letters.'

'You had better be careful Casanova,' teased James, 'Remember how Danny sent Joy's letter to Mavis and they both turned up to the dance that Saturday night?'

The boys had a good laugh remembering what they called the comedy of letters. The boys passed the stairs leading to the Health Department, then under the canopy that led to the administrative offices. Henry was the first to reach the communication section. He hurried to the alphabetically pigeon holes and picked up a handful of letters and examined them.

'McDonald, McIntosh, Mendonca, Mingo,' he repeated as he sorted the letters. 'Major, yes this is it,' he said joyfully as he took his letter.

James was beside him carefully examining the letters with the initial 'C.'

'It is from Essequibo, stamped at the Bartica Post Office. At last a letter from Jackie!' Henry said delightedly. 'Boy, I can't wait to read it! Hurry, James let's go!'

'Not so quickly,' said James, 'I haven't found my letter yet.'

'What!' said Eddie, 'but Shelly said that there was one for you and she was pretty sure about that.'

'Probably she was mistaken,' Henry said.

'No way, that's not like Shelly. She would have sneaked a peek at the handwriting to ensure that it didn't look like a girl's handwriting,' Eddie said jokingly.

'Someone, maybe Alva or one of those guys may have taken it to your room believing that you were in the dormitory,' suggested Henry.

'No one has ever done me such a favour.'

'Maybe Shelly was joking,' suggested Eddie. 'Anyway run along to your room and see if it's there.'

'We will try to get Shelly,' said Eddie.

James raced out of the office, hurried past the multipurpose center and under the rain-protecting canopy leading to the boys' dormitory. He scrambled up the stairs to the second floor where his room was located. As he ran along the corridor heads appeared from behind sliding doors wondering if there was a disturbance somewhere in the building.

'What's the matter?' asked Mr. Simon, as James swung open the door of room 507A.

'I'm looking for something, Mr. Simon,' he answered breathlessly, closing the door noisily behind him.

James cherished his letters. He knew that they were something of value to appreciate for students who were living away from home or soldiers on deployment. It was a symbol of pride and belonging. The importance of receiving mail from home or a special someone was priceless. Gossip was often spread about those who received mail regularly and those who didn't. Terry Kissoon in the male dormitory and Cynthia Cummings in the female dorm were believed to have been sending themselves letters to be a part of the in group. No one was certain, but rumors and gossip traveled faster than the truth.

James rushed to his table. It was just as he had left it that morning. He lifted the reading lamp, seeing a brown piece of paper. It was a brown envelope and on it was marked, 'CONFIDENTIAL—ON GUYANA GOVERNMENT SERVICE'.

He sighed with relief as he picked it up, but, it was opened. His heart skipped a beat. The envelope was roughly torn open and to his utter dismay the contents were missing.

James stared unbelievingly at the opened envelope. The person who had done this favour had done so purposefully for different intentions. He gripped the damaged envelope tightly and hurried back along the corridor.

A HELPFUL MR. SAM

Henry and Eddie meanwhile had gone in search of Shelly, but she had left the Design and Technology Department after submitting her assignment to Mr. Green. They asked some girls if they had seen her and they were directed to the social studies and humanities room.

When they got there Shelly was deep in conversation with her two best friends, Anita and Abiola, known to her friends as Abi. Anita Applefarm was Eddie's girlfriend and Abiola Clarke, who was James' cousin, was closely attached to Henry. The three girls looked up when they heard the approaching footsteps.

'Hi girls, planning a picnic for us?' Eddie joked.

'No, nothing of the sort,' answered Anita.

'We're just discussing what we can do to keep you three out of trouble,' Shelly said worriedly.

The girls, especially Abiola, were always concerned about the boy's welfare and many times they succeeded in talking them out of daring adventures.

'Where is James?' asked Shelly. 'Reading the letter he received, I think.'

'We are not sure about that,' said Henry.

'What's the matter with you? You seem so worried, not your usual selves. Is something wrong?' asked Shelly.

'Yes, indeed you all look nervous,' added Anita.

'Do we appear so?' Henry wanted to know.

'Sure you do,' said Abiola, nodding her head in agreement.

'If I didn't know you, I would have said that you were about to rob a bank or do something really dreadful,' said Anita.

'Did you hear that we were entertaining a few other guys up here?' Shelly said teasingly.

'No! Nothing of the sort, we know you guys too well to entertain such thoughts,' Eddie laughed light-heartily.

'Okay, enough of the wise cracks. Our real intention for checking you out is to inform you that James' letter is missing,' Henry said.

'Missing!' they chorused simultaneously.

'Don't get worried,' Eddie cautioned. 'We don't know if someone has taken it to his room. He has gone to check. He should be here soon,' he added to reassure the girls.

'Then let's meet him downstairs,' suggested Abiola, showing immediate signs of concern.

'Excellent idea,' Anita and Shelly agreed.

The girls collected their books and together with Henry and Eddie they left to meet James. They found him as he was leaving the art room where Aubrey, Brian and Clinton were working wonders on their canvases with paint splattered brushes. Without greeting the group he held up the envelope before their eyes.

'Thank heavens you found it,' said Shelly, hugging James and giving him a kiss on the cheek.

'Don't be too excited,' he told them. 'I found the envelope, but the contents are missing.'

'What!' said Henry, as the others looked on in utter shock and bewilderment.

They were certain that this had never happened on campus before, and it was often mentioned at general assemblies that the personal property of all must always be respected.

'Do you mean that someone has taken out the contents?' Eddie asked disbelievingly.

'Exactly, that's how it appears to me,' replied James, lifting the lid of the torn envelope.

'Who can be so cheeky?' asked Abiola.

'Whoever he is deserves to be expelled from this institution immediately,' Shelly said angrily.

'I have no idea who could have done something like this,' admitted James with a forlorn look.

'You seem so cool about this serious affair,' observed Anita.

'Did you expect this letter?' asked Shelly.

'No, I have never received any official Government stamped letter before,' James said showing them the officially stamped envelope.

'Wow!' said Henry. 'You are sure important. I am proud to have you as a friend,' he said trying to inject some humour into the conversation.

No one laughed and Anita said, 'Why must such things always have to happen to you boys? Trouble and misfortune seem to be following you around. Only this morning Henry was nearly killed, now a stolen letter,' she ended magnifying the morning's mishap.

'It is not our fault,' Henry answered her, 'it's probably because the Lord knows that we are fully capable of handling such situations that he is constantly putting us under tests of this nature,' said Eddie his high cheek bone rising as he feigned a smile possibly thinking that his humorous remark would ease the tension.

The remark passed and Abiola asked, 'Have you seen Mr. Sam yet?'

'No,' James answered, 'not about this particular incident.'

'Then you should do so now before this gets worse,' she advised with concern within her voice.

'Right, off we go to Mr. Sam's office,' agreed Henry, leading the way.

James tucked the envelope into his pocket and found another piece of paper there. He took it out and looked at it. It was the piece that he had found in the education room after the shade had fallen. For a moment, he thought he recognized a pattern among the mysterious petroglyphs, but he was mistaken. A dark cloud seemed to drift across his brain. He gently pushed the paper back into his pocket.

The group reached the administrative building and the girls decided to wait outside while the boys spoke to Mr. Sam. Mr. Sam's secretary, Miss Abrams was not in the office so the boys approached the principal's office which appeared to be open.

Although the door was opened, James knocked then waited for the deep guttural voice to invite him in.

'Good day boys! Two visits in a few hours,' said Mr. Sam as he got up and extended his hand to James. Henry always noted that no matter how many times the boys visited Mr. Sam, he would always greet them warmly as if seeing them for the first time.

'How are you Henry, James and Eddie?'

They acknowledged that they were in good health. It was truly amazing that Mr. Sam remembered the name of every student on campus.

'Sit please and make yourselves comfortable,' he said nodding to the chairs in the center of the office.

'Thank you,' they said as they eased themselves into the comfortable arm chairs constructed of local yellow silverballi and simarupa.

'So boys what's the nature of your second courtesy call?' he asked jokingly. 'Problems with your classes or grades?'

'Not at all Mr. Sam; our classes and grades are all good,' said James who usually acted as spokesperson for the trio.

'That's good to hear, I expect no less from my students, and you are here to succeed. That's your primary and foremost purpose at this institution,' he added.

'Our reason for seeing you now is to report a serious incident,' James said.

Mr. Sam sat upright when he heard James' statement.

'It concerns a stolen letter,' continued James.

'A fallen shade and now a stolen letter. Is that right?' Mr. Sam said showing the noticeable confusion in his voice as he rubbed his bald head and adjusted the bows of his spectacles.

'Yes sir, the first as you know is about that broken electrical shade in the education room and now the second is about a letter that was sent to me. It appears my letter was stolen,' James informed the baffled principal.

With the aid of Eddie and Henry, James recounted the details of the broken shade and the stolen letter as best as they could. They later told the principal they assumed these mysteries could be connected.

'Very interesting,' said Mr. Sam, 'the shade could have been an accident but the letter, I can't understand who could have taken it.'

'Any of the one hundred and twenty-eight of us living in the male dormitory,' said Eddie.

'This is really disgusting,' said Mr. Sam.

'What I cannot understand is why someone had to steal this letter!'

'The letter could have been very important,' said Henry.

'If it wasn't important, it wouldn't have come in a stamped Government envelope,' said James.

'Do you mean it had the Government Seal?' asked Mr. Sam.

'Yes, here is the envelope,' said James taking it from his pocket and handing it to Mr. Sam, who again adjusted his glasses.

Mr. Sam took the envelope and carefully looked at it, searching for all details. 'It was posted on the 23rd of . . .' he paused then continued, 'I cannot see the month, but, it was sent from a postal outpost in the Essequibo region, it looks like Dawana!'

'That sure gives us a lead,' said James. 'We can contact all the Government Offices in the Essequibo and try to locate the person who sent it.'

'That would be quite a task,' said Mr. Sam thoughtfully.

'I know it would be difficult,' said James, 'but it can be done, after all, it's our only clue.'

'James is right, Mr. Sam. We can use three different telephones. Divide the Essequibo County into three regions and let each person investigate one region,' said Henry.

'Excellent,' added Eddie, 'I have a brother who is a detective corporal at the Aishalton Police Outpost. He'll be willing to assist us.'

'You boys talk like detectives,' said Mr. Sam.

'We are amateur detectives,' James informed the Principal, 'but we usually work under cover.'

'Do you mean that you have been here as police spies?' asked Mr. Sam. 'And to think that I trusted you!'

'Don't be worried, Mr. Sam,' James said trying to calm him. 'We are not police spies. We worked on small cases like recovering lost articles and there was the time that I helped my uncle with one of his cases.'

'You had me scared,' admitted Mr. Sam taking out his white handkerchief and wiping away imaginary beads of perspiration from his nose and forehead.

'Does that satisfy you, Mr. Sam?' asked James.

'Yes, it does,' answered Mr. Sam fumbling in his cigar case for a tension breaker. He took out a long Cuban cigar and held it between his fingers without lighting it. He never smoked in the presence of students.

'Then would you allow us to do some investigations on this case?' asked James.

'Yes, of course you have my fullest cooperation; do all you can to solve these mysteries boys. I'd like to know who the misfit in this institution is. Remember to always be extra careful and safe.'

'Could you tell us the Government Offices found around Aishalton area, Mr. Sam?' asked James. 'We can begin our investigations from that point.'

Mr. Sam began naming the offices he knew along with some assistance from Eddie.

'Hold on, not so fast,' begged James. 'Let me write down the names of the offices for future reference.'

James pushed his hand in his pocket and pulled out a piece of paper he had picked up in the Education room. Without James saying a word, Mr. Sam, who noticed the mass of jumbled shapes on the crumpled sheet said, 'Let me see that paper,' he requested.

James handed over the paper. He looked at it from above his glasses. The boys eyed him eagerly. His countenance changed from one of deep concentration to one of total amazement. 'My goodness, where did you get this from?' he asked.

'I found it with the broken glass shade,' James told him.

'How did this get here?' asked Mr. Sam.

'No idea,' the boys mumbled, baffled at Mr. Sam's sudden expressions.

'These are representations of the Petroglyphs discovered in the interior. Copies are found at the museum and the archives.'

'Do you mean the Timehri Rock Paintings?' asked Eddie.

'Exactly, the Timehri Rock Paintings date back to prehistoric times and are found throughout North and South America and Central America in countries like Chile, Peru, Bolivia and Brazil and countless others.'

The boys listened attentively to this amazing story. 'The Government has employed anthropologists to decipher these curious symbolic representations. There is a Culture and Research Station located in that area,' said Mr. Sam.

'Do you think the letter and this note can have any relation?' asked Henry.

'It's possible,' said Mr. Sam. 'As far as I know, there is also a postal outpost in that area.'

'This is getting more interesting and complicated,' said Eddie.

'But, how did this reach the Education Room?' asked Mr. Sam.

'More questions than answers, at this time,' said James, 'as is always the case.'

'Very philosophical,' said Mr. Sam. 'The only difference is that you will have to supply the answers. My brain is too old for such fatigue. Go right ahead and try to solve these mysteries; you have my fullest cooperation and whole hearted support. You will have the use of all the telephones and radio sets, cameras and other equipment you may need to assist you. If there is need for transportation, my Forbes Lotus and the minibus are always available.'

'Well thank you, Mr. Sam,' Henry said. 'We had better get going, it's lunch time.'

The trio thanked Mr. Sam again, shook his hand and left. When they departed his office, they discovered that the girls had left, so they hurried to their rooms to prepare for lunch.

A NARROW ESCAPE

L unch was eaten in the multipurpose hall where the boys queued up with the other students and slowly advanced to collect their meals. When they reached the counter, they eyed the different varieties of dishes. During this time of the day the smells of numerous Guyanese dishes wafted the air. Everyone knew the wonderful smell the cooks provided without the bells needing to announce its presence.

'What shall I eat today?' James wondered out loud. He noticed someone in front of him order pork fried rice and a side dish of stewed bora with fried tilapia.

'What are you eating?' James asked Henry, who was behind him.

'I'm undecided, what about you?'

'I don't know, the metagee looks great, the pepper-pot smells delicious, and then there is stewed bora and cook-up rice. I just can't decide.'

'What about you, Eddie?' asked Henry.

'No need to ask, you know Amerindians can't bypass pepper-pot,' Eddie said, smiling.

'Any cassava bread to go with it?' teased James.

'No, pepper-pot is all I need for today.'

'I think I'll try the metagee,' said James.

'I will try the bora stew,' Henry decided.

Their minds made up, they requested their meals. A dark-skinned beauty flashed a smile, as she handed Henry his meal.

'Anything more?' she asked politely.

'Yes, a glass of warm milk and some custard,' Henry told her.

Henry's order met, he proceeded to the dining hall. Eddie was next, as James had exchanged places with him.

'And you?' she asked Eddie.

'I'll like pepper-pot.'

'And for dessert?' she asked.

'Some ice cream, a piece of fruit cake and can I have a glass of tamarind juice?' answered Eddie.

It was now James' turn to be served. The young cafeteria assistant flashed a smile at James and asked him what he would have for lunch. James looked deeply into the brown eyes and returned the smile. She blushed.

'What would you like to have?' she asked, her voice sweet and melodious.

She would make a very good model, James thought, 'I'll like two things.'

'What are they?'

'The first is your name, and the second is a plate of metagee.'

'Call me Tekla,' she said smiling, as she handed him his meal.

James wanted to prolong the dialogue, but someone at the back shouted, 'James we're hungry and you're keeping us back, get going.'

James appeared discouraged. *Why must people always try to impede my progress*, he thought. The girl was new and he was trying to make a friend to increase his chances of being served quickly when he was late and extra portions to take up to his room for after hours.

'Kindly pass me some milk and a bit of sugar. I'll see you later,' he said winking at her, as he received the milk and sugar.

He joined Henry, Eddie and the three girls in the dining hall. As usual, the inseparable six were lunching together. The atmosphere was alive with conversation, every member of the staff and the entire student body ate together. There existed in the college a rare and enviable unity and understanding that was fostered by the principal and entire staff.

Mr. Sam had done a lot to integrate a loving brotherly and sisterly culture into the college program. He was the architect of change, a man loved and respected by all. There were trying times, but his motto of 'per ardua ad astra: through difficulty to the stars,' he said, kept him focused and led him through difficult periods. He said openly that his motto was borrowed from Tutorial High School and said that if something is useful we must always use it to our betterment and never to our detriment.

The six chatted about the meeting with Mr. Sam. 'So we can have the minibus for ourselves?' asked Abiola, who loved picnicking and sightseeing.

'Not, in that sense, my dear,' James told her, not wanting her to be carried away by the idea of six young people, roving the coast from Lake Mainstay on the Essequibo to No.63 Beach on the Corentyne, picnicking and holidaying.

'Do you mean that only you boys can use the mini-bus?' she asked feeling slightly hurt.

'You misunderstand me, Abiola.'

'I understand you perfectly! To infer that in this egalitarian society, men are more equal than women,' she countered. 'Is this egalitarianism; is this in keeping with the total liberation of our country's women?'

'Abi will you listen to me?' said James slightly annoyed, knowing she got this way when she could not have what she wanted.

'All right, let me hear your excuse. A lame excuse is a man's only defense,' she said indignantly.

'You are right, but the women believe the lame excuses, so who is wiser?'

Everyone loved when the two cousins got into playful disputes. They argued about religion, politics and various societal issues. Their friends knew they never tried to hurt each other but at times it was entertaining listening to their arguments.

Abiola did not answer. She looked across the table at Eddie who was busily putting spoonful after spoonful of food into his mouth and then at Shelly who was gazing at James.

'Continue with your excuse, James,' she said, 'I'm listening.'

'As I was telling you, the minibus was only promised for us to use in solving these two mysteries. Do you understand now?'

'You win. Anyway I'm terribly sorry, I had misunderstood you,' Abiola apologized.

They continued talking idly as they ate their meal. Later, they switched to making plans for the afternoon. The girls decided to visit a friend from Trinidad who was staying at the luxurious Pegasus Hotel. The boys decided to rest for the Annual Football Match which was to be played for the Prime Minister's Trophy.

The trophy had been won by the powerful university team the two previous occasions. Another lien on the trophy and it would be with the university, 'for keeps.' The coach had therefore urged all team members to rest two days before the match and engage in light exercises and mandatory physical exercises in the mornings and afternoons.

Shortly after lunch, the boys saw the girls off to the Pegasus and they went to their rooms to rest. The trio slept longer than usual. Henry was the first to awaken. He looked at James, then to his wrist watch. The luminous numerals indicated that they had overslept. It was approaching eight o'clock. He tugged James. 'Roommate,' he said as James sat upright, 'I am afraid we have missed dinner.'

James rubbed his eyes then snapped, 'you mean that we will have to go hungry?'

'Not if we can collect something from the girls or from the warden. If they have, we will get it,' said Henry.

'Let's make a call to the girls dorm then.'

'Fine, let's get going.'

They hurried to the telephone and rang the girls but they were out of luck. They then phoned the impartial mother-substitute of the resident student, only to learn that they were again out of luck.

'We will buy some biscuits and cheese,' Henry said, as he hung up the receiver.

'Eddie is still sleeping,' noted James as they passed his room. 'We will just have to wake him when we return.'

The two boys collected some money from their room and left. The night was unusually dark and cloudy. They had to follow the white dividing line on the driveway. Occasionally, candle flies provided them with an inadequate supply of light.

They walked in silence. Suddenly, out of the still night they heard the roar of an engine. It was a car; they could not estimate its distance because the headlights were off. They immediately stopped, turned and walked in a right angle until they touched the soft grass. The beat of the engine was getting louder. The car was coming toward them.

'I wonder who is that madman?' asked Henry.

'His lights have probably failed.'

'But it's getting closer and closer, and we can't tell its speed nor can we locate its position in this darkness.'

The lights of the car suddenly went on. It was approximately fifty meters away. The glare was blinding for Henry and James. Their eyes were not accustomed to the sudden brightness. When the car increased its speed the boys could not see anything and the danger they were in.

The two beams of light were penetrating their eyes, and they shielded their eyes with their hands as the car bore down on them. It was only twenty-five meters away. The driver was deliberately trying to run them down. Their only escape was in the muddy ditch nearby.

'Dive James, dive!' shouted Henry hastily and in panic as they plunged headlong into the ditch.

The car missed them by mere centimeters. They were covered from head to toe in mud and slush. They struggled out of the ditch clawing their way up the embankment as the car turned and sped into the night. They had absolutely no time to identify the color of the car, its model or license plate.

The incident took less than twenty-seconds but it seemed like a lifetime.

THE NIGHT PROWLER

Henry and James hurried back to the dormitory all muddy and foul smelling. They walked the entire way to the light under the stairway leading to their rooms on the second floor without a single sound. This was to make sure no one heard them and also because they were shaken up with this sudden brush with death. They both decided against ascending the stairway and dirtying their rooms.

'Eddie,' Henry called from outside.

Luckily, Eddie had awoken, he peered outside. 'My gosh!' he exclaimed. 'What in the name of peace were you two up to?' he asked.

'Just went swimming in the shallow water,' answered James jokingly.

Heads peered out of the louvers at the wet and foul smelling boys.

'Look at a couple of mud hogs,' Robert shouted, laughing as he surveying Henry and James through the open louvers.

'Don't leave us here to rot,' pleaded James, wiping away the mud from his forehead.

'All right, we'll give you a helping hand,' said Jack, a student living across from Eddie.

Coming to the muddy boys help were Eddie and Jack. The two boys had more help than they needed. Miss Lyle, the warden, had followed the growing stream of students and had found herself in the inner circle surrounding the shivering muddy boys.

'Isn't there enough water in the bathroom for you two?' she asked.

'Yes, Miss Lyle, I suppose there is,' answered Henry.

'Then why go swimming in the muddy water? Do you realize the danger to your health?'

'We did not go swimming,' James answered apologetically.

'Then how did you get into this messy state?'

'We were on our way to buy biscuits for dinner,' James began.

'Then what, did your money fall into the mud?' interrupted Jack, a student on their floor.

'No, not at all. We were run down by a car,' said James.

'What!' Miss Lyle exclaimed astounded.

The boys told the warden about their narrow escape much to the amazement of the other students. 'You boys seem accident prone,' she hinted. 'It's terrible; we will need extra protection for the compound. I will have to speak to Mr. Sam about a few extra guards. Then the police must be informed, we cannot tolerate such outrageous attacks on students. First, we have to wash you two up.'

'Yes, let's use the fire hose,' suggested Jack with excitement.

'An excellent idea,' complimented Miss Lyle. 'That will save you the trouble of having to clean the bathroom.'

The bath, with the fire hose, turned out to be the most exciting Henry and James ever had. Water was squirted all over the lawns and many times they had to seek shelter when the would-be helpers turned on the hose to its maximum.

After the bath, Henry and James, followed by Eddie, hurried to their room to change their dripping clothes. The water began dripping faster as they ran up the winding stairs, leading to the second floor. When they reached their room, they found to their utter dismay, the door was bolted from the inside and the lights turned off. Henry lifted the door and shook it to unfasten the bolt. Suddenly, they heard muffled sounds inside the darkened room.

'Someone is in there,' Henry whispered.

'Yes, I heard a sound too,' said Eddie.

'Open up, we are freezing,' James shouted. There was no reply. 'Whoever is in there open up before we break in, that is our room you are in,' said James, as he pushed himself against the door and tried to unbolt the door.

With James finally giving up, Henry and Eddie tried frantically to unbolt the door, but to no avail. James went down on his knees and peered through the slanted wooden louvers. He saw a short figure removing the louvers from the window. The man had a scarf around his nostril thus concealing his identity.

'Let's break in,' whispered James.

Time was running out. The boys had to act immediately or else the suspicious character would disappear into the dark night. Together, they rushed towards the door and leveled their shoulders against it. It flew open but the intruder had probably anticipated this act, and he struck the remaining panes violently with torchlight and heaved himself through the remnants of the jagged frame. As he jumped on the zinc canopy, the boys noticed that his left hand was cut off at the wrist.

They ran to the window and followed but he ran along the canopy and jumped to the ground. The trio was in hot pursuit. The intruder was about twenty-five meters ahead, as the boys jumped on to the slippery turf. He was heading northerly in the direction of the university's campus. On the left of the campus was a large enclosure consisting of fruit trees, wild bushes and vines. Eddie was walking over to the university library one day when he discovered that summato, monkey apple and gooseberry were found there in abundance.

If this man reached this wooded area, he would surely be well concealed and their chances of catching him would be gone. The boys were breathless in trying to overtake this unusually swift one handed prowler and were within a few meters of him when they reached a long narrow bridge over the canal separating the college from the university.

The man gained the slender structure and started to hurry across. The pursuing boys were just behind, inching closer and closer. Suddenly the man stopped, turned back and shook the slender structure violently. The trio was taken by surprise; they had not anticipated such an action.

Henry, who was in the lead, stumbled and fell forward. Losing his footing he had to desperately reach to cling onto the greenheart crossbeams that supported the bridge. Henry thought of how unlucky he was and scared for his life dangling from a bridge in total darkness. He knew precious seconds were ticking away and the prowler was capitalizing on this delay. He could clearly hear the prowler's footsteps taking him farther along the rocking bridge.

Henry could notice James leaning forward and extending his hand for him to hoist him back on to the swaying structure. When Henry had regained his balance and composure they continued the chase, but valuable distance now separated them from the fleeing figure.

'Keep going,' said James. 'We'll catch him.'

'He'll head for the trees,' said Eddie shouting back to James, who was still helping Henry.

'Good, when we reach dry ground, we'll split up and try to encircle him.'

When the boys noticed the man had reached the other side, he took out a torchlight and beamed the light into their faces. 'Go back and don't try to follow,' he shouted in a hoarse voice.

'Ignore the threat,' whispered Henry 'let's try to keep him talking.'

'Go back or you'll get hurt,' said the one-handed intruder.

'We'll capture you, and then go back,' answered James, trying to edge his way towards the end of the bridge.

'You boys know too much! We'll get you all right,' said the man in his grunting voice as he continued to shine the torchlight on the boys.

'What do we do know?' asked Eddie.

'This is the last time I am telling you to turn back! You shouldn't poke your nose into what doesn't concern you. Turn back or I'll stone you.'

'We won't turn back until we capture you,' replied James.

'All right,' said the croaking accentuated voice. 'Take these with the compliments of Alfie Walcott!'

Alfie Walcott as the man called himself, bent down and with his one hand began hurling stones and other missiles at the boys mercilessly.

The trio was in a very difficult and tenuous position. In front of them was a one handed maniac, throwing rocks and stones at them, under them a narrow and swaying bridge, and below a 30 meter wide ditch. The light was blinding, making it impossible to see the flying objects, many of which fell into the ditch and splattered them with mud and grime.

Walcott laughed as coarse raindrops began to fall on the boys. The boys knew that the night was worsening for them much to Alfie Walcott's advantage.

. The boys could do nothing and wondered how a man with one hand could produce such a rapidity of fire An object struck James in his face; he groaned and groped in the darkness for support but found none and fell into the ditch. There was a tremendous thud as he fell and Walcott laughed gleefully. He then beamed his light on the struggling James.

'See you brave little boys,' he said, 'I must be going. I have a date with the boss; you'll get the chance to meet the two of us one day.'

A huge grey cloud with arms like an octopus blotted out the moon and even shadows were obscured. Alfie Walcott turned off his torchlight instantly and peppered the darkness with objects. Eddie and Henry could do nothing to stop the fleeing Walcott, who within a few seconds was within the dense enclosure, free from all possibilities of capture.

'What luck!' exclaimed James, as he was helped to firm ground by his two friends. He wiped away the mud from his forehead and added, 'This Walcott character is really mean.'

'Wonder what he was after in our room?' Henry asked.

'Save the questions, we can figure the answers out when I'm home and dry.'

The unlucky trio retraced their steps to the college compound. Miss Lyle was more than furious. She bawled her head off, when she was again confronted by the muddy boys. 'Why didn't you apply to enter the Fishing Industry before trying for college?' she said furiously.

'It was an oversight,' mused Eddie, 'our applications probably got misplaced.'

'Cut out the back chat and cheeky talk!' she shouted. 'How can you like to be so dirty and stink?' she fumed, 'We should bury you alive instead of washing you again. What is the excuse this time?'

'No excuse Miss, I just fell overboard while chasing a prowler out of our room.'

'Don't come a step closer to me! Are you sure it was overboard or was it into the cesspit?' she said covering her nose from the foul stench.

'No, it was a real thief, a one handed prowler,' added Eddie.

'All right I'm tired of you three, I'll see you to your rooms after you've cleaned off that mess; and you about a one handed man, and you had better stop visiting the Strand cinema. I've been hearing about all these Chinese movies that are corrupting you young people, Enter the dragon, The one armed swordsman, Bruce Lee, Chen Seng, Wang Yu are all a bad influence,' she said, pointing to Eddie.

'No, Miss Lyle it was a real prowler with two feet and one hand,' put in Henry.

'Don't be funny Henry Major,' Miss Lyle said. Henry smiled; he wondered how Miss Lyle knew the names of the major actors and the movies. She must be a very big fan of the karate and kung-fu phenomenon sweeping the country.

The boys were again washed, but this time under the watchful eyes of the warden. When they were clean, she followed them to their rooms. 'How in the name of peace did this happen?' she asked shaking her head sideways.

Room 507A was in shambles. The door was broken, glass was splattered over the floor and the lockers were ram-sacked. The boys explained what had happened. Miss Lyle was aghast. 'You boys are in great danger,' she said. 'You can't sleep in this room tonight; you will have to stay with Dr. Prass.'

Dr. Prass was the resident doctor. He was a pleasant character, so the boys welcomed the idea. Miss Lyle helped them clear the room of the debris then took them to Dr. Prass' quarters. Dr. Prass was not on the campus so the boys remained with Miss Lyle until he returned.

When the doctor returned and had garaged his Burnham Special, he went to Miss Lyle's quarters for his usual evening chat. He met the boys, who were playing chess. Henry was about to be checkmated by Eddie. James had earlier conceded defeat to the crafty warden. Dr. Prass greeted them and Miss Lyle explained what had happened. He listened carefully, nodded his agreement then left shortly after with his two charges.

It was late and neither Miss Lyle nor Dr. Prass wanted to wake the principal but the boys knew that both of them would submit written reports to Mr. Sam first thing in the morning. They again recounted their encounter with Alfie Walcott over coffee and sandwiches and shortly after, the boys retired to bed after a most hectic day.

EDDIE TAPES A MESSAGE

They had a comfortable night's rest and were only awakened when the dormitory bell rang at five thirty. Today was to be a very important day in college life. It was to be the day on which the college football team was to try to wrest the Prime Minister's Cup from the powerful university squad.

The entire football team was exempt from the compulsory agriculture program which was structured in keeping with the Government's 'Feed, Clothe and House the Nation' policies. The sixteen members of the team took breakfast under the watchful eyes of their coach, Señor Pablo Tostao, a former Brazilian world cup star who was working as an Education Attaché at the Brazilian Embassy. The university team on the other hand was being coached by Graham Kavanah a former Manchester United star now working as a Volunteer Service Officer with the British Consulate and seconded to the University of Guyana.

It was a long day, probably the longest the students had ever experienced. The match was scheduled to start at 4:30 p.m. At three, the university supporters began arriving. In half an hour the college campus was transformed into a carnival city. The lawns were barricaded just leaving enough playing area. The eastern and western stands were filled to capacity.

At 3:45 p.m. a Government Transport Vehicle arrived with the university team. The university supporters went wild. They raised totems and flags, waved them wildly and sang choruses for their team. The team disembarked, much to the delight of their fans and the other spectators and was cheered on to the field. Suddenly, there was a tumultuous roar; the college team was making its entry.

Thousands of hands and heads rose simultaneously and the college supporters drowned the cheers from the opposing quarters.

Both teams took to the field for warm up and this sent the crowd into a frenzy. The university team ran to the western end of the field and started shooting the ball around and engaging in the normal bending and loosening up exercises. The college team did a slow lap around the field to the enjoyment of their fans. The atmosphere was intense and electric. Spectators had come from as far as Mahaicony on the East Coast, Peter's Hall on the East Bank and Vreeden Hoope on the West Bank. Dignitaries arrived and took up their seats amidst clapping and cheers. Food and fruit vendors formed a virtual ring around the spectators. Today was a special day with lots of black-pudding, egg ball, cheese roll, pine tart, roti and curry, cookup rice, channa; you name it and it was there.

It was four twenty-five; five minutes to game time. The players were making their grand entrance. Eddie, who was not a regular player, sat ten meters from the touch line, 'To victory, to victory,' he shouted as Henry and James appeared. The players walked single file to the center where the ball had been placed and were presented to the Chancellor, who also booted the ball to mark the commencement of the game. A massive cheer went up when the ball was formally brought into play. Doris, the university center forward, passed a long smooth pass to the inside right who sent a high pass down the right wing. The pass was intercepted and won by the college midfielder; he weaved past the two university forwards, cut to right and sent the ball to James in the center. James controlled it skillfully, pushed it with his right foot to the inside left, Browne, who ran down the wing. The college supporters went wild. 'Shoot, shoot!' they shouted.

Browne hesitated momentarily and two university defenders sandwiched him and brought him down. The referee blew the whistle for a foul. The Training College camp was agog; they had a free kick just outside the penalty box. This was dangerous! Browne was to take the kick. He eyed the ball then moved in to strike, it was a hard, straight right footer! A good shot! 'Goal, goal!' the G.T.C supporters shouted in anticipation, but the ball hit the crossbar and was booted away by the university defense. The shouts died woefully. The game had indeed gotten off to a good spectacular start.

The match proved to be a grim tussle with both teams carrying out periodic raids on the other's goal. At half-time the score board read G.T.C nil, U.G. nil. The second half started with the same quick, fluent display of ball skill by both teams. Twenty minutes into the second half the university players were visibly tired so they brought on two substitutes. The college supporters sensed this and began a morale boosting chant. The team reacted superbly. The ball now seemed to be always with the college players and in the university's goal area. Frantic struggles were waged, but all the college's threats of scoring were repulsed. The college employed a new line of attack, playing seven forwards. The university had nine of their players in the penalty area.

On one such occasion, when the college was carrying out one of its raids, a university defense player smashed the ball outside the struggle area, towards the center. The college defense was stranded. It was a race to reach the ball first. Two university players out ran the field and pounced on the sphere menacingly, showing superb control and acute ball mastery and skill.

The college pavilion was immediately transformed, from a tumultuous carnival-like spectacle, into a pondering solemn arena, hopefully anticipating the bitter end, the imminent humiliation and death of their champion matador, and much more, the sun that was ever so tantalizing took to its heels and hastily sought a moment's cover behind a thin white cloud. A white and grey bird, a chicken hawk, lazily flew by, but asserted its course and speed, on hearing a distant chirp and perceiving the hurrying form of its tormentor, a much smaller winged creature, a kiskadee. The university player shot to goal, Henry dived, but too late, the ball ripped into the far corner of the net. The university had scored.

'The university had scored!' The university supporters cheered wildly. The college supporters were astounded. Their exuberance and joy were dampened by the ball at the back of the net. Many college supporters, rather than witness the on field celebrations of the university players, dejectedly walked to the bathroom or grabbed a welcome snack.

Just then, it was announced over the public address system that there was a call for James Clarke. James was occupied on the field of play and could not have possibly responded to the call, so he asked Eddie to take it for him. Eddie hurried to the phone on the western side of the multipurpose hall. On his way he heard a multitudinous yell of 'G.O.A.L, G.O.A.L!' and the clanging of chairs as the mammoth crowd leapt into the air. From the massive uproar he knew that the college had scored the equalizer. He was tempted to hurry back but the thought of missing the call prompted him on. He reached the booth and picked up the receiver.

'Hello, Cyril Potter College of Education' he said.

'Is that James Clarke?' a masculine voice asked hastily.

'No, James is involved in a very important football match at the moment,' Eddie explained.

'Can't he spare a minute?' asked the caller. 'This is of the greatest importance, please see if he can make it, please,' begged the caller.

'No Sir, he just can't afford the time now, if you call back in fifteen minutes you'll be able to speak to him. The match should be finished by then.'

'This is a long distance call, it would be very difficult for me to phone again, you know how these lines are, they just go dead at any moment!'

'Where are you phoning from?'

'From Dawana.'

'Is that so?'

'Does it surprise you?'

'Indeed, we seem to be coming across that name rather often. A letter addressed to James and stamped in that area was stolen a few days ago,' he further explained.

'My goodness, stolen, stolen, but it was a registered letter and it carried the government's seal. I posted it myself!' the caller blurted out.

'In that case James can know what the contents were, if you are the person who sent it.'

'That letter is of the greatest importance, is it really lost?'

'Yes it is, what's your name, may I ask?'

'Hugh Joseph Cheong,' was the answer over the phone.

'Are you Hugh Cheong, the famous Guyanese archaeologist and anthropologist?' asked Eddie. 'The person who is in charge of National Archaeological Surveys?'

'Yes, I am,' said Mr. Cheong.

'James should hear of this, but he just can't make it now. The entire college is at this moment depending on him to give them a long awaited victory.'

'Stolen, the map, the key to wealth untold in the hands of unscrupulous thieves. Would they destroy the secrets of the Timehri Rock Paintings and the archaeological data that I have strived all these years to decipher?' said Hugh Cheong, rather in soliloquy than to Eddie.

'Listen. We don't want to waste precious time, these lines are known to go dead any moment. I have a miniature tape recorder I'll insert it to the earphone and give you five minutes to say everything you know, including the contents of the stolen letter and your possible suspects and I'll give the tape over to James just after the match is finished.'

'Can I trust you?'

Eddie sensed the vagueness and absurdity of the question, but did not prolong the dialogue. He ascribed the question to the psychological strain that Mr. Cheong had evidently gone through.

'Yes, you can.'

Eddie inserted the tape recorder and settled down to await the expiry of the allotted time. In the distance, he heard the distinct calls to both teams to press on; however he had no idea of the score. He knew that the university had scored the first goal, but then, there was the goal he presumed was scored as he was on his way to the telephone. For the first time since final examinations, had Eddie looked at his watch so expectantly, and imploringly. 'Hurry up and go around!' he shouted, at the crawling minute hand. It ignored the harsh command and the second hand continued its pedestrian journey.

He looked away to the west and saw the sun had changed into a dark golden disc against the sky and envisaged its similitude to the yolk of an egg in a pan of hot coconut oil. He glanced again at his watch; three minutes had elapsed. He eyed the receiver in his hand and was tempted to eject the tape. Two minutes seemed like a life time. He began counting the seconds as they limped by. His eyes momentarily glanced to the fields around; he saw a stallion eagerly attempting to mount a mare. Such was life! He eyed his watch again and realized that the five minutes had expired. He removed the tape from the earphone and listened, the line was dead! 'I wonder if anything is on the tape?' he wondered, as he replaced the receiver and rushed back to view the closing stages of the game.

Exactly two minutes remained. He glanced at the score board, it read Training College—one, University, one. The spectators were on their feet, the game was tense and all eyes were glued to the field, all ears were deaf to the other's remarks and all hearts were pounding as the greatest piece of machinery strove to supply its various owners with the much needed red fluid.

The ball was with the university forwards who were visibly playing for time, employing freezing tactics, round about dribbles, short passes and kicks over the touch line. They were not even trying to advance; all they had to do was to force a draw to retain the Coveted Cup. Ninety-seconds to go and the countdown had begun. Under pressure a university defender wisely booted the ball over the touch line. One minute to go, the college left back Jerrick took a throw from the touch line way into the university half. The ball was collected by Rogers who sent a pass to Gomes, Gomes cut in and over chucked to Jerrick, Jerrick on the right wing was sandwiched and brought down. The ball was booted out of the danger area towards the centre. The college goalkeeper ran forty meters to the touch line and passed the ball to James. This was dangerous play no one was in the college area even the goalkeeper was advancing making an all-out bid to score. The referee took a cursory look at his watch as the university supporters shouted for him to blow the whistle. He could not, since there were still twenty-seconds to stoppage time.

The ball was with James on the centre line. All the college players were moving forward like soldiers on the march. In the university half, all their players fell back to defend. James still had possession; he sent a pass to the unmarked Rogers. Three university players tackled him but he managed to cross to Gomes on the right. The crowd was alive and vociferous; they sensed danger in the closing seconds of the game. The college goal was without a goalkeeper, he was also in a striking position. Twelve seconds to go and the referee took another glance at his watch. The ball was passed to Rogers, who was rushing in. He flicked it over to James. It was high, but James out jumped two university defenders and headed to Gomes. Gomes passed to Rogers. The university players were confused. The college players had been practicing this style of play all season. It was called the Round Table. Ten-seconds to go and the college players still had possession of the magic sphere. Suddenly the Round Table opened and a player with the ball rushed menacingly forward. It was James. He out maneuvered the university defense and kicked to the goal. The Shot was low and well placed. It ripped into the far corner of the net, leaving a prostate goal keeper and ten bewildered losers. The whistle blew, the match was over! James had scored in the last second of the game.

The crowd invaded the field and the college super-heroes were lifted triumphantly off the field. They had finally done it, they had wrested the coveted cup from the university. Sweet revenge for the humiliating defeat they had suffered after a six goals to nil drubbing by the university last year. The coach took them to the locker room where a few speeches and toasts using nonalcoholic beverages. There was absolutely no drinking on campus as most of the students were under the legal drinking age. When all the formalities of the victory were completed the players returned to their adoring fans. It was now an open celebratory party with music and dancing and everyone knew it was a start to a wonderful evening for everyone at the college.

AN ELUSIVE SUSPECT

The girls found them and guided them away from the raucous crowd. One of their often quoted sayings was taken from Auntie Cumsie who advised women and girls to 'never leave your man when there is music, dancing and other women around, ahem mark carefully what I Auntie Cumsie say now.'

The boys acceded to the girl's wishes and were taken to one of the quiet areas reserved for teenaged after hour trysts. James and Henry were in a cheerful mood still savoring the victory and relishing the praises heaped on them by their significant others when Eddie remembered the telephone conversation and the taped message. He brought the others up to date and when Mr. Cheong's name was mentioned the others were astonished.

It was Abiola who first voiced her amazement. 'Hasn't he been awarded the Golden Arrow of Achievement?' asked Abiola.

'Yes, so you see, if he has been writing James, it's possible that he is in line for the Caciques's Crown,' said Henry looking teasingly at James.

'Yes, if I get the Cacique's Crown, I bet you'll get the fool's cap,' said James laughing.

'Okay guys it's much more serious than that, you see, Mr. Cheong spoke about wealth and secrets of the Rock Paintings and such the like, I couldn't take all in this already packed storehouse I have for a head, so I told him to put it on this miniature tape recorder,' said Eddie as the others listened attentively. 'So you see on this little thing, we have all the information, come on let's listen to the play back.'

'Good work, but we have to seek a better place. We could have eavesdroppers, you know,' suggested Henry.

The two footballers returned to their rooms changed hurriedly and with the others left for the Social Studies Block. The crowd had thinned appreciably but the motor cars were still slowly winding their way out from the parking lots.

'There is your roommate Eddie,' Shelly said pointing towards the flow of departing cars. 'The entire afternoon he sat at the rails talking with that strange character he is now seeing off.'

'Why do you say strange? Does he look that different?' asked James, throwing his arms around Shelly's shoulder and fondly cuddling her.

'Well, he just looked that way to me, it is not often that you see a one-handed man around these parts you know,' she added with a shrug of the shoulder.

'A what?' asked James stopping in his tracks. 'Did you fellas hear that?'

'Sure we did!' they answered.

'Can he be Alfie Walcott?' asked James.

'It's possible, so let's follow him' suggested Henry.

'No, you are not sure,' said Anita.

'That's true,' added Shelly. 'He may even try to harm you if he is the one you encountered the other night.'

'Anita's right, you can approach him politely and ask his name, if he says he's Alfie Walcott, you can contact the police,' said Shelly.

'I think you ought to follow him and see what he's up to,' suggested Abiola boldly.

'Abi's right,' said Eddie.

By this time, the car with the suspect was worming its way towards the main entrance.

'He has a car, how can you catch him?' asked Eddie.

Anita was searching for all the possible ways of preventing the boys from following the suspect.

'We'll follow him! Henry get the keys for the minibus from Mr. Sam,' said James.

'It's out of order, gone for repairs, I think,' said Anita.

'Oh my goodness! What shall we do?' asked James.

'Simple, ask him for his car,' suggested Abiola.

'Good idea,' said Eddie.

'Abi, keep this tape safely until we return. You can also tell Mr. Simon and Miss Lyle that we went after a suspect,' said James.

The green Guybrand Vauxhall with the suspect was approaching the main highway. James and Eddie started at a fast run to cut the distance between them and the car, but the traffic had eased and the green Guybrand Vauxhall was moving at a faster speed.

Meanwhile, Henry had found the cooperative principal, and after hastily giving him the necessary explanations, he collected the keys for his Forbes Lotus.

'Take care of yourself,' Mr. Sam called after Henry.

Henry swung open the door of the car, and instantly started the white sports model. It was the first of its kind assembled in Guyana. He drove to where the three girls were standing peering alarmingly after the striding figures of James and Eddie.

'Where are they?' he asked as he slowed to a virtual stop.

'Running ahead,' answered Abiola. 'Do drive carefully!'

Henry swung the car on the driveway and raced towards the exhausted two. 'Hop in guys,' he said as he pulled up. 'Which way did he go?'

'He's heading towards town and is probably seven hundred meters ahead,' James panting informed him.

'Okay, strap on your seat belts and let the best driver in town catch that one-handed intruder,' said Henry.

Henry chucked the Lotus into the fast flowing Georgetown traffic.

'Hold your horses and take your foot off the gas. We don't have goggles,' said Eddie with a worried look on his face.

'Use your hand as wind breakers,' suggested Henry.

'Slow down, Henry!' said James. 'In this way we may overtake the suspect without even realizing it.'

'All right chicken-hearts, a green Guybrand Vauxhall up ahead,' said Henry.

'Good work, get closer and keep him in sight,' said James.

Henry overtook two crawling Hibiscus Specials and pulled behind a Guyana Co-operative Sugar Estate truck. The sugar truck turned into the Sheriff Street leaving the Lotus exposed. The Guybrand bearing the suspect turned into Kitty, swung into Barr Street, then out into Vlissengen Road. The boys kept it in view. It stopped at Vlissengen Road and Church Street Traffic light. The trio had no alternative but to pull up behind.

'Check the number,' Henry advised.

'That's done already,' said James 'GUY 14 RG. It was bought recently, I should think about last week judging from the number.'

The boys sat back to avoid recognition. 'It's too late' said Henry. 'I'm sure he spotted us as we moved in. He's been glancing suspiciously into his rear view mirror for the last few seconds.'

The light changed and straight away the suspect swung his car into North Road at an incredible speed. Henry was a bit slow, not in the least anticipating this hurried departure.

'It's Walcott all right,' said Eddie, as Henry negotiated the corner.

Walcott was ahead by twenty meters. The famous Bourda Cricket Ground appeared diminutive as the white Lotus shot by. Walcott turned recklessly into Albert Street then out into Regent Street, his tires screening and smoking. The boys followed. Pedestrians hurriedly leapt on to the pavement for safety and traffic literally stopped. Heads and sulky faces grimaced after the two speeding cars.

'All yu tink dat dis is South Dakota race track!' a man selling shave-ice shouted.

A pastor on the sidewalk made a hurried sign of the cross and mumbled. 'Youth is speed. Father forgive them, for they know not how dangerous it is.'

Even Bourda Market and its bustling crowd seemed insignificant. The cars were approaching Camp Street, the lights up ahead changed indicating caution, then stop. Walcott gripped the steering wheel with his one hand, pressed the gas to the floor, driving recklessly through the traffic signals. Cars slammed their brakes noisily to a standstill. Two cars shed their wind screens into the air in a splattered mass of flakes and broken glass. Henry brought the Lotus to a halt inches from the automatic controller.

'Walcott has slipped through our fingers,' said James.

'More than that, he has left us in a real mess,' added Eddie.

The drivers were scurrying out of their cars and examining their damages. Some were even advancing menacingly towards the boys.

'We'll never catch him now,' said Henry.

'It's hardly likely; there are so many places he can go. Searching for him would be like searching for a rat in a rice field,' said James.

A siren sounded above the hooting horns indicating the police were making their appearance.

'We'll have some questions to answer,' said Eddie. 'Not right now, they will have to sort out this traffic jam and then look after the accidents before coming to us, I hope no one is seriously injured.'

'We could have been injured if that cop hadn't stopped those chauffeurs,' said James.

Four traffic officers alighted and began directing the flow of cars and other vehicles. A burly inspector motioned them to the corner. 'You lads will have a few questions to answer, we heard that you started it all.'

They refused to comment.

'First dangerous driving; we got a report from an outrider,' he added, as he retreated towards the other police officers who were taking statements and making measurements.

A truck from Singh's Cooperative Enterprises arrived and began to ferry away the damaged vehicles.

'It's your turn now,' the inspector said, 'I think you'll have to accompany us to headquarters, but first, let me get the names, addresses; you know the procedure don't you?'

'Henry Major, age seventeen.'

'Student or working?' asked the inspector.

'Student teacher at Turkeyen Campus,' answered Henry.

'And you! Student teacher too?'

'Yes, I'm James Clarke, age eighteen, address Turkeyen Campus.'

'Are you Clarke?' asked the inspector, looking directly at him.

'Yes.'

'Any relation to Supt. Clarke at headquarters?'

'He's my uncle,' James said showing some signs of worry on his face.

'Should have guessed as much, could have passed as your father, such striking resemblance and you?' he asked pointing to Eddie, 'Kaie's direct descendant, I presume.'

'Not at all, I'm a proud Macusi, Eddie James is the name, eighteen years.'

'Good, Corporal Gifford, bring the vehicle forward,' said the inspector, his face jumping as he spoke.

'Who's the driver of this?' the inspector further questioned, pointing to the Forbes Lotus.

'I am,' answered Henry.

'Alright, follow us to headquarters,' the inspector said, as he entered his vehicle.

'I didn't know that Supt. Clarke is your uncle,' said Henry.

'He's such a famous detective there is hardly anyone in this country who doesn't know about his reputation,' added Eddie.

'He's my uncle all right, but that doesn't mean that it would get us out of this spot,' said James with a serious expression on his face.

MEETING SUPT. CLARKE

After a five minute drive, both cars pulled up inside the police headquarters compound.

'Sorry I didn't introduce myself before, I'm Inspector Jordan. I work along with your uncle,' he said, 'Corporal Gifford you can patrol the Albuoystown area with Constables Salim and Blair.'

'Follow me,' the inspector ordered, turning militarily and making long crisp strides towards a winding stairway. 'This will take us to the sixth floor where our office is found. I prefer to walk rather than use the elevator you know. The exercise is good.'

'It's not often that we have the opportunity of ascending such high buildings. Other than the exercise, it will be an exciting and new experience for us,' James assured the inspector.

'There is also the opportunity to see the various departments first hand,' said Eddie.

'Who knows, later we may be serving Guyana from within these walls!' added Henry prophetically.

'You may soon be serving years behind bars for all those traffic violations that you have committed,' teased James.

'If that is my lot, I accept it with open arms,' answered Henry.

'This section should interest you. It's the Criminal Investigation Department or CID. On the right is the photography section, then, that is the finger print and handwriting detection department. I started my career in that section,' the inspector informed them.

Inspector Jordan at last reached a glass cubicle with the names Supt. Clarke and Inspector Lennox Jordan inscribed on name plates above the door.

'Here we are boys,' he said. 'We are lucky to find the busy Supt. Clarke in office.'

They entered. 'Didn't expect you back so early, Lennox,' said Supt. Clarke rising slowly.

Supt. Clarke was a slim middle-aged man greying at the side burns. He got up from his desk slowly still looking at a pile of papers on his desk.

'I didn't myself,' said Inspector Jordan, 'if I hadn't encountered these lads, I would have still been out along Main Street or in the Kingston area.'

For the first time, Supt. Clarke looked at the boys, his eyes shifted from Henry to Eddie, then to James. 'If it isn't my scholarly nephew, I'll be damned!' he exclaimed. 'How long I've been trying to contact you my boy?' Supt. Clarke hugged his nephew, 'I have a little surprise for you! I bought a new car and because Tony is too young, I'm handing over the Tapir Special to you. All the papers are already in order.'

'Thank you very much uncle! Abi will be delighted when she hears of this,' said the jubilant James.

'You mean when she sees it. You're taking it back with you when you're leaving today.'

The others listened as the two Clarkes enquired about how James was adjusting to living in the dorms. He assured his uncle that all was fine and that he had adjusted well. The preliminaries completed, Supt. Clarke said, 'You know my colleague, Inspector Jordan, I think.'

'Yes, of course, and these are my friends, Henry Major and Eddie James,' said James.

'Glad to know you boys,' said Supt. Clarke shaking their hands. 'Make yourselves comfortable; let me get something for you to drink.'

Supt. Clarke pressed a buzzer and a constable appeared. He requested coconut water. The police officer disappeared and later returned with large tankards containing the appetizing liquid. Supt. Clarke asked how the boys had met Inspector Jordan. Inspector Jordan gave a graphic account of the meeting.

'You have violated the traffic regulation, have you realized that? Speeding along the busiest roads in the country, you could have added a few deaths to the already high road fatality,' said Supt. Clarke.

'We were shadowing a crook,' said Henry in defense.

'A crook?' asked Supt. Clarke rather dubiously.

'Yes, a one handed man who entered our room and stole a very important letter and stoned us,' added Eddie.

Inspector Jordan and Supt. Clarke leaned eagerly forward.

'A crook, a one handed man?' asked Inspector Jordan.

'It's true, let me explain,' said James.

'The mystery began with Henry nearly being struck by a falling electrical shade. Later we found a piece of paper with queer unintelligible signs. The Principal, Mr. Sam later described these as ancient Amerindian rock writings taken possibly from Tramen in the Upper Mazaruni.' James further explained that a letter addressed to him was stolen and told of Eddie's telephone conversation with Mr. Hugh Cheong, the archeologist.

'Sounds interesting and dangerous business to me,' said Supt. Clarke.

'But how you boys come to be involved in this affair?' asked Inspector Jordan.

'I'm an amateur detective,' said James toying with the collar of his shirt playfully, 'other than that I don't know.'

'You have the making of a good detective,' complimented the Superintendent, 'but let us hear some more about this crook you were after.'

'This is more than you boys can handle,' interrupted Inspector Jordan. 'This matter should be left to us. What do you say Chief?'

Supt. Clarke looked at the three youthful faces, whose wide eyes showed that everything depended on his decision. 'I think we can leave this to James and his crew. Let's see how they'll handle their first case, we'll give them the necessary cooperation and assistance.'

'Thank you for having so much confidence in us,' said Eddie.

'We can surely handle this, Supt. Clarke,' added Henry. 'First, you can process these pictures of Alfie Walcott. I took them when he stopped at the traffic lights.'

'Now, I'm all confused again. You lads do work quickly! Now who's this Walcott character?' asked Supt. Clarke.

Here, Henry took up the story and told the baffled officers of the one handed stone thrower who called himself Alfie Walcott. He finished by telling of the car chase after the football match and the eventual chase that landed them at police headquarters.

'You say Walcott had a green Guybrand Vauxhall. That's a good lead. What's the number?' asked Inspector Jordan.

'GUY 14 GR,' answered Eddie.

'Good, we can check that out with the Registration Office. We may be able to get valuable information from there,' added Inspector Jordan.

The trio waited patiently as the inspector radioed the Registration Office.

'Yes, this is Inspector Jordan, C.I.D. Can you give me details about a green Guybrand Vauxhall number GUY 14 GR . . . Thank you, I'll hold.'

'We seem to be getting somewhere, if we can trace the owner of the car we may find out more about Walcott,' said Henry.

'Indeed, and the mystery can be over if we can get Walcott to talk,' added James.

Supt. Clarke pulled a cigar from a silver case and lit it thoughtfully.

'Have you boys started smoking yet?' he asked. They answered in chorus a resounding no. 'Good, it's a bad habit you shouldn't pick up.'

Inspector Jordan held the receiver to his ear while Supt. Clarke puffed thoughtfully, the smoke forming a spiral as it ascended. There was a long silence only broken by the ticks of the clock as it edged its way towards six o'clock.

Inspector Jordan received the much awaited call. 'Yes, Inspector Jordan here, speak a bit louder please,' he yelled into the mouthpiece. 'What did you say? Stolen? Thank you.'

He hung up the telephone and said, 'Let me have one of those cigars, Patrick.'

He lit the cigar then began pacing the room. 'We're back to zero. The car Alfie Walcott was driving was reported stolen by a Jairam Tiwari from Lusignan.'

'This Walcott is indeed desperate,' said Supt. Clarke as he picked up his short wave radio. 'Headquarters to all patrol cars. Report stolen green Guybrand Vauxhall. Number GUY 14 GR. Locate and report to headquarters immediately.'

'What about the photographs?' Henry asked. 'We may get a good lead as to the identity of Walcott.'

'Sure, that shouldn't take too long,' said Supt. Clarke taking the camera from Henry. 'You lads possess more guile and cunning than I thought. Follow me,' he told them, as he got up and left his cubicle.

They made their way to the Photographic Section where Supt. Clarke handed the films to a Corporal to process. 'You can take a look around, the inspector and I will be back in a few minutes. Also, feel free to ask questions lads,' he smiled as he and the inspector left.

'Thank you,' they called after the officers. Fatigue overwhelmed them and they slumped into arm chairs to await the return of the Photographer, Inspector Jordan and Supt. Clarke. 'The best thing that happened today is the car I've got,' said James.

Meanwhile at Turkeyen, Abiola, Shelly and Anita were eagerly awaiting the boys' return. Shelly was in her room looking at a picture of James she kept on her writing desk. She was anxious for him to be back. Since the boys were taking a long time to come back, she worried that they ran into some danger. She picked up the framed portrait and ran her fingers around the cheeks. She pulled it to her breast and softly, in soliloquy, whispered, 'James, I do love you. Wherever you may be at this moment, take good care of yourself, my love.'

There was a soft breeze blowing against the louvers. She stretched out her hand and released the catch; a mild wisp reached her face. She looked outside. From her room, she had a commanding view of the lawns, the driveway and the boys' dormitory. All the rooms but one was lit, she knew that room was James'. He was away probably far away with Henry and Eddie.

Unknowing to her, Abiola and Anita were making their way to her room. They stopped at the warden's quarters and told what little they knew and left. Abiola was clutching a straw shoulder bag. The bag contained the taped message James had given her for safe keeping. They reached Shelly's room but it was closed. Abiola tapped softly and Shelly heard the knock. It startled her and she quickly replaced James' photograph on the table before opening the door.

'You gave me quite a scare,' she said bashfully as she opened the door.

'Is that so?' asked Abiola, taking a seat on the edge of the bed. 'We thought you were asleep.'

'No, I was thinking about the boys.' She admitted.

'Or, was it about him?' Anita asked, smiling and pointing a finger at James' picture on the table.

'Your lips look wet, have you been stealing kisses from my cousin?' teased Abiola.

Shelly blushed and refused to comment.

Back at Brickdam, the photographer was handing the developed negatives to James when the officers returned. Unfortunately the pictures were poorly taken and nothing could be seen.

'It's getting late uncle, so we have to be going now,' said James.

'We'll keep in contact with you. By the way, here are the keys for your car James. I'll get two outriders to accompany you.'

After a few minutes all was ready and the two cars, James' gift and Mr. Sam's Forbes Lotus, left under escort for Turkeyen.

EDDIE IS CAPTURED

Reaching Turkeyen, the boys waved goodbye to the police escort and turned into the college compound. They parked the cars and hurried over to the female dormitory.

'Hi girls,' they beamed as the girls rushed to meet them.

'Thank God you're all in one piece!' said Anita.

'See! Nothing to fear! We can take good care of ourselves,' Eddie assured her.

'Where's the tape?' asked James.

'Just here, safe and sound,' said Abiola handing it over.

James gave the girls an account of the afternoon's proceedings, mentioning, much to their delight, the gift he had received from his uncle.

'Did you get any food for us? We are starving!' said Henry.

'Of course we did,' answered Shelly.

'Then please let's have it, my belly's grumbling,' said Eddie.

'It's upstairs, I'll get it,' offered Anita.

Anita soon returned with three lunch containers and a flask of tea.

'What can a man do without a woman?' asked Abiola.

'Don't mention it, I might be tempted to try it!' answered Eddie.

'Have a good night's rest lover boys,' they called as the boys departed.

Henry hardly waited; he began opening his food container even before he reached his room. Eddie and James did likewise. Before they had reached their rooms, they were half way through their dinners. Fifteen minutes later they were filled and brushing their teeth in the washroom.

'We'll tackle that tape when we're finished,' said James. 'We don't know what's on it and before it's stolen or misplaced I want to get that information in my head!'

'Good idea, but I'm not game, I'm much too tired,' said Eddie.

'Tired doing nothing?' said Henry.

'Yeah, if I don't get enough sleep I wouldn't be able to eat as much as I would like tomorrow night.'

'Oh yeah, that's all you think about, that long elastic tummy of yours,' teased Henry.

'Want me to think about you, friend? Right now I am thinking about some good sleep. After all tomorrow will be the closing party and you know, I must be there,' said Eddie. 'See you in my dreams, that's if you pass my way. Goodnight heroes!'

'So that's it. We'll have to work on the tape alone,' said James.

'No harm, Eddie did his part by getting it in the first place.'

It was fast approaching midnight. Henry and James were at their desk with the tape.

'Can you hear anything?' Henry asked.

'No, nothing so far.'

'But this tape has been running for three minutes.'

'How long did Eddie say he gave Mr. Cheong to speak?'

'Five minutes, can't we have a bit more volume?'

'No, nothing more this is not a juke-box you know,' James replied jokingly.

Suddenly, they heard a faint voice emitting from the tape.

'Something is coming,' said Henry, his face brightening up.

'Be absolutely quiet.'

'Can I trust you?' was the barely audible plea.

They waited a little, but heard nothing more. Then they heard the voice say, 'Captain Persaud, Captain Persaud XRG 58 HT.' They listened but that was all. The tape had been run through.

'What a weird message?' observed Henry. 'Is that all or have we missed some parts?'

They played the tape over, but that was all.

'Let's figure it out,' said James. 'We have one slender clue, 'captain.' It can be a boat captain, a captain of the National Service or the Army or even the Salvation Army.'

'You can have so many Captain Persauds that it would be useless going in search of one.'

"The XRG 58 HT.' What can that be, some kind of coded message?'

Tried as they could, they could make nothing of 'Captain Persaud, XRG 58 HT.'

'One thing I'm sure about, it's not the number of any motor vehicle or it would have been GUY,' said Henry.

'What about a boat or airplane number?'

'That's possible, what if we start investigating at the Wharves tomorrow?'

'Fine, it's time for bed. Tomorrow we start, I wonder if Eddie has started dreaming already.'

'See you in the morning pal,' Henry said as he tucked his head under his blanket. Within a few minutes both of them were snoring or as Guyanese say 'pulling timber.'

✱ ✱ ✱

Wonder where Bollers is? Eddie thought as he put on his pajamas and climbed under his blanket. Within a few minutes Eddie was fast asleep and dreaming as usual. He was a regular dreamer, strangely however most of his dreams revolved around food. There were times when he was dreaming about attending Muslim and Hindu weddings and being loaded with Indian dishes by the hosts. There were other times when he dreamt of being awarded first prize trips to the National Food Centre. Tonight however, he was the owner of a restaurant and today being his birthday, he was being entertained by his employees. He was about to receive a bowl of chicken soup when he heard someone entering the room. Rudely awakened, he inched the blanket from over his eyes. It was his roommate Denny Bollers. Eddie noticed Bollers head to his locker and taking out a packet and torchlight.

Eddie watched him carefully while feigning a few snores. *Wonder what Bollers is up to at this time of night,* he thought. Bollers appeared to be staring at him to see if he was asleep. To Eddie Boller's actions were strange since he turned and tiptoed out of the room, carefully and noiselessly closing the door behind him. Eddie thought he should follow him.

As he pushed his blanket aside he thought about waking Henry and James but decide not to. He decided he would tackle this one alone.

Barefooted, he tiptoed at a safe distance after Bollers. Because the dormitory doors were locked to prevent intruders Bollers had to extract a few louvers on the ground floor and without replacing them climbed through and vanished in the darkness. Eddie on his hands and knees followed, but soon lost sight of Bollers in the darkness.

Eddie then noticed that Bollers had reached the stairs and flashed the torchlight along the corridor to see if he was being followed.

'I can't give up now, he is just up ahead,' he mumbled to himself.

He stopped and listened. The night was dark; no stars were in the sky. The moon was behind a barricade of grey clouds. Weird forms began taking shape on Eddie's mind. It was a good night for baccoos, jumbies and dopies to roam and he was not the bravest of boys. He was tempted to turn back, but then he heard distant voices.

What is Bollers up to, he thought.

He crept closer. In the darkness, he now saw three men. He concealed himself behind some black sage trees. The men were talking, but, he couldn't hear clearly, only a few mumbled deeply accentuated words.

'But Blackie, the boss said,' one voice began.

Eddie crept nearer and nearer.

'The plane should be here anytime now,' said Bollers.

'So Bollers is mixed up in this business,' he said to himself. 'Wait until Henry and James hear of this!'

'It's time to take up positions,' said Blackie, 'Ginger, remember twenty paces east, Bollers are you ready?'

'Yes, I am and remember no torches until the plane is six hundred meters away,' said Bollers.

Wonder what they are up to? Eddie also thought he could jump them but that wouldn't be the best thing, since they may be armed and they outnumbered him in any case.

He strained his eyes in the darkness as the three figures turned on their heels in different directions making long deliberate strides. In the distance, he heard a sound, it became clearer and clearer. It was a plane. When it was about six hundred meters away he saw three flash lights flicker in the darkness. Bollers and his accomplices were in a triangular pattern and they were obviously signaling to the aircraft. Up above he saw a green flare. Signals were flashed from below at regular intervals as the plane dived lower and lower.

Eddie knew the plane couldn't possibly land but wondered if they were planning to collect something.

It was indeed a drop, for when he looked keenly he saw a parachute floating gently down. The three signalers pounced upon it as it touched the ground. They were working in absolute darkness. Suddenly, he heard voices behind him. He was caught between two forces. He couldn't move forward, he couldn't go back.

'Have matches, Antonio?' a voice asked roughly.

'Yes, here,' was the reply.

There were two persons. 'Light this cigarette for me, you know my hands bother me, Antonio.'

Antonio struck the match. Eddie gazed in horror. It was Alfie Walcott with another man and both were carrying revolvers. Walcott saw the kneeling figure and shouted to Antonio.

Antonio responded instantly and beamed a torchlight on the helpless crouching Eddie. Eddie saw death staring at him out of the barrels of the two revolvers. He raised his hands over his head voluntarily.

'What's happening Walcott?' asked Bollers and he and his accomplices burst onto the scene.

'Blasted nosey kids,' said Walcott. 'The boss would be pleased that we have nabbed this one.'

So Walcott's not the boss, thought Eddie, *I wonder who is?*

'What must we do with him?' Antonio asked quietly to the others.

'Can't take any chances we don't know if he's alone and how much he knows,' murmured Walcott.

'Yeah, his two pals may be lurking nearby,' said Bollers.

'In that case we have to put him to sleep for a while,' said Walcott, 'or he may shout for his two pals.'

Blackie and Antonio held Eddie's arms in a vice like grip and Walcott with the butt of his revolver registered a bone cracking blow at the back of his head. Eddie lost consciousness, a huge gashing wound at the back of his head.

THE MESSAGE IS DECIPHERED

Morning reached too quickly, as far as Henry and James were concerned. It seemed as though they had five minutes sleep instead of five hours. 'Wonder what that lazy Eddie is doing,' said Henry, 'just making his final turn in bed I bet.'

'Let's wake him up and tell him about the message that he taped.'

'I've heard that early to bed early to rise makes a man healthy, wealthy and wise.'

'It's the other way around with Eddie, makes him lazy,' added James jokingly as they strolled along the corridor to Eddie's room.

Eddie was not in his room. 'Wonder where the guy has gone so early?'

Eddie's roommate Denny Bollers was fast asleep and snoring.

'May have gone to the bathroom.'

They checked the bathrooms and toilets but found no trace of their pal. 'Probably he's in the Physical Education Room or in the weightlifting room,' suggested James. 'That's not like him, he has only gone to the gym two times for the entire term. Anyway let's not panic, this may be another of his jokes or disappearing acts.'

'Fine, let's see what will happen at breakfast.'

At breakfast there was still no sign of Eddie. They told the girls that Eddie was missing and Henry implored them to keep it a secret until they did a bit more investigating.

'Don't go around spreading it; we sure wouldn't want the entire college to panic. If that happens it will upset all our plans,' advised James.

'Okay we will keep our mouths sealed, but hurry up and inform the police,' suggested Anita.

Not one of the five ate a hearty breakfast. They all sat dejected and very worried a part of them was missing. The normal jovial mood was gone until Anita broke the silence. 'By the way have you anything?' she inquired.

'No, he was still asleep when we came down to breakfast,' Henry answered.

'We had better have a word with him,' suggested James.

'We'll keep you girls informed and do remember don't mention Eddie's disappearance to anyone,' added Henry.

They hurried upstairs to Eddie's room where they found Bollers packing to leave campus.

'Leaving today Bollers?' James asked him.

'What's that to you, and why shouldn't I leave?'

'Nothing, but why not remain for the closing dance tonight? You know that it's a college tradition,' Henry chipped in.

'I'm not in the habit of sporting, dancing and such nonsense,' snarled Bollers, 'After all unlike you I have a home and a family I can go to.'

James ignored the terse and insulting remark. He looked Bollers directly in the eye and asked him when last he saw Eddie.

Bollers looked at James with scorn and loathing. 'What's that to you, I thought that you were a student, not a private eye,' he said.

'That's a question Bollers, it deserves an answer,' James said.

'I don't like supplying answers,' Bollers retorted, 'so leave my room before I throw you out.'

James took two menacing steps towards Bollers. 'Want to try that Bollers?' James asked as Henry stepped in to block the door.

Henry sensed that Bollers knew he was outmatched. Bollers tried taking a step back.

'Let me also remind you Bollers that I am the dormitory student representative and I have the authority to enter any room to inquire about anyone living in this building. So, supply the answers or else.'

Henry, seeing James clenching his fist like a boxer, decided to take up this threatening position too.

'Okay loudmouth, you win this round. The last time I saw him was when I went to bed, he was fast asleep and snorting like the bauxite train at Ituni, anything else?'

'Yeah a lot more, I think that you're lying, so you had better start over,' he warned the visibly shaken Bollers.

'I'm telling you all that I know and that's the truth, now get out of my room,' said Bollers but not with any conviction.

'All right, you win the first round just like Lennox Blackmore, but let me tell you, Beckles will be back for the second," said James drawing an analogy about two of Guyana's most illustrious and famous boxers.

Frustrated and dejected the boys proceeded to Mr. Sam's office. Luckily, the principal had arrived early for work. They returned his car keys and told him what had transpired. They gave a detailed account of the car chase and their visit to police headquarters at Eve Leary. When they mentioned Eddie's disappearance he became visibly concerned and paleness enveloped his normal jovial demeanour.

'Why did this have to happen on the last day of the term?' Mr. Sam wanted to know.

Henry and James had no answer. They looked at Mr. Sam as he adjusted his spectacles, then extracted a Cuban cigar from a silver case, which he had no intention of smoking. Mr. Sam was confused and beads of perspiration appeared on his forehead. He took out a white handkerchief from the pocket of his jacket and daubed the beads away which were streaking down his face like rain drops on a window pane.

'We'll find Eddie soon,' they assured him, but Mr. Sam seemed unconvinced and had a faraway look in his eyes.

Henry signaled James, using one of their secret codes, that it was time to go.

'Can we have two of the college's short wave radio sets?' requested James. 'They will help us immensely in our investigations.'

'Yes, you can collect them from Mr. Simon.'

Mr. Simon had overall responsibility for all the male students and equipment on campus. The students referred to him as the campus police.

'Thank you, and we'd also like to make some phone calls,' said James.

'You are welcome boys, and whatever else you need know that the college's resources and equipment are at your disposal.'

The boys again reassured Mr. Sam that they would locate Eddie very soon and bring the entire episode to a conclusion. They knew that Mr. Sam was not convinced and they too had no idea how they would find their beloved colleague and friend.

They found Mr. Simon in his office and informed him that Mr. Sam had given permission for them to use two short wave radio sets. They collected the radio sets and were very relieved because Mr. Simon did not ask any questions. They set about making the phone calls; the first was to police headquarters.

'Hello uncle,' James said as he recognized his uncle's voice. 'Have you been able to get any information about Alfie Walcott?'

'Nothing so far, but I have two detectives working on the case.'

'It seems as though Eddie was possibly captured. He just disappeared without leaving any message or anything. He may be injured or even killed,' James informed him.

'I'll detail some detectives to investigate,' promised Supt. Clarke.

'Uncle, concerning Mr. Cheong's message, all he said was 'Captain Ernest Persaud, XRG 58 HT,' a bit strange; can you make any sense of it?'

'The Captain Persaud can be any of a few hundred persons, boat captains, prison officers, police officers or army officers.'

James agreed and realized that it was a dead end. 'But uncle, what about the number XRG 58 HT?'

'That's right, it sounds like an aircraft registration number.'

'So it seems.'

'Let me call Camp Ayangana, stay on the phone. I have to use another phone.'

As James waited for his uncle, his mind wandered about Camp Ayangana. It was the National Army Headquarters and was located on the edge of the City of Georgetown, facing the famous seawalls and the Atlantic Ocean. He remembered seeing the immense seawall that was first built by the Dutch in the 17th Century when they ruled parts of then Guiana

He thought Guyana was unique in many ways, as Mr. Simon always said. Since it is six feet below sea level, the building of the seawall along the coast and the erection of kokers to control the floods and to keep out the raging Atlantic Ocean has been necessary. Guyanese slaves under the leadership of Cuffy led the first successful slave rebellion in the Western Hemisphere at Fort Nassau on the Canje Creek, Berbice in 1763. Guyana can also boast of having once been ruled by the French, Dutch and English and being influenced also by the Spanish. The influence of these cultures on the nation is seen by such village names as Uitvlugt pronounced (I-Flock) and Sparendaam (Dutch), Hopetown and Stanleytown (English), Chateau Margot and La Bonne Intention (French), Santa Rosa Mission and Anna Catherina (Spanish). James was always proud of his country and pondering the uniqueness of his country served a good escape in such stressful times.

Supt. Clarke returned from the adjoining room, picked up the telephone and continued his conversation with James. 'Just as I thought, the XRG 58 HT is the registration number of one of the helicopters presented to the Guyana Government by the British Government. The helicopter is used by the army,' said Supt. Clarke.

'Thank you very much Uncle Patrick, this information is very useful. I will contact someone at Camp Ayangana and will keep you informed about developments.'

'Now we are getting somewhere,' he said turning to Henry. 'The XRG 58 HT is the serial number of one of the Defence Force helicopters. Uncle Patrick just checked it out.'

'And these radio sets, what are we going to do with them?'

'Oh these, we will use for communicating when you are in Mr. Sam's car and I will use mine. We'll scour the town looking for Eddie or signs of him, we'll use the radio sets to keep in contact with each other.'

Five minutes later Henry and James left the college campus en route to Georgetown.

✱ ✱ ✱

Eddie woke up to find himself in a small dark room. The bleeding had stopped, but there was great pain. 'Where am I?' he asked. He tried to move but his hands and feet were tightly bound. Through a small barred window of the room, a streak of sunlight entered, lending some cynical comfort to his confused mind.

'Well, at least I am alive,' Eddie murmured as he tried to comfort himself.

'He's awake Blackie,' a rough voice shouted.

Eddie peered into the darkness in the direction of the gruff voice but he could see nothing since the streak of light that had given him a glimmer of hope was now gone.

'Then put the blind fold and gag back on,' was the harsh reply.

A piece of old cloth was shoved into his mouth. 'Antonio, what about the blindfold?' Blackie asked.

'No need for a blindfold, no one will find him here, but if they do, he'll be long dead and our mission will be completed by then. Dead tongues don't wag, so whatever he sees or hears he can't repeat,' said Antonio.

Eddie was totally helpless; moreover, he was both hungry and thirsty. His mind was troubled. What of his friends at Turkeyen? Were they safe or were they also kidnapped and have found themselves in the same predicament? Would he see them again? If he died, would he be found and given a decent burial? He twisted his hands and his feet to slacken the knots but the knots were expertly tied. He pulled his mouth along the foul smelling room to ease out the gag but it was too far in and he was choking. His mind was in turmoil. The heat and stench of the room was sickening. Apparently, Blackie and Antonio were using a corner of the small room as a toilet. Perspiration streamed from his forehead unto his face and into his eyes. The salty liquid burned his eyes and he was disappointed that Blackie did not put on the blindfold.

'Antonio, call Walcott on the radio and inform him that Bollers isn't here yet,' Blackie instructed.

When Eddie heard the name Bollers he wondered if it was his roommate and how he was tied up with such a group of criminals and crooks.

Antonio obeyed and took out his radio set, 'wolf to agouti, wolf to agouti, are you receiving me, over.'

'Loud and clear, over,' came the cackling reply.

'Leopard hasn't arrived yet, the horse is harnessed and in its paddock. When must the birds fly?' Antonio asked.

'When Leopard arrives and horse is shot,' said Walcott.

'Is that all? Okay over and out,' ended Antonio as he tucked the radio set into his pocket.

'Heard that amigo?' Antonio asked standing over the bundled mass of flesh in the center of the room.

Antonio raised his foot and pressed Eddie's head painfully into the ground. Eddie grimaced with pain. He was in great agony. Antonio then kicked him flush in the face. Blood streaked from his eyes and nose. At that point Eddie thought that he was at the point of death.

'Lay off the kid Antonio!' Blackie shouted with obvious disgust and disdain at his accomplice's cruelty.

'Soft hearted, eh Señor Blackie? I am a mercenary, I must be tough,' he said as he chewed on a piece of tobacco.

Eddie detected a distinctive Spanish accent but could not decide whether it was South American or Central American. The pain was too much for him to worry about accents.

'Yeah, Antonio you are paid to kill, not to kick wounded helpless boys,' said the enraged Blackie.

'Mi amigo, I don't kick often. The last hombre I kicked was my father. He was dying. He called me a murderer, poor fool.'

'Bastard, and you're proud about that! You don't have a conscience; no self-pride and your heart is made of stone,' said Blackie scornfully.

Henry knew then that he was truly in deep trouble when Antonio replied, 'Si amigo, I am prouder than you think. I would never help foreigners to over-run my country for money, hear that amigo!' Antonio shouted, 'You help to destroy Guyana for a few lousy pesos!'

'Shut up you blasted Spanish pig,' bawled Blackie. 'The boy is hearing us.'

'Of what use can there be of his knowledge, amigo?' laughed Antonio. 'Wouldn't he be dead in a few minutes when Bollers arrives? Dead hombres tell no tales.'

Eddie listened aghast. He had valuable information, but there was no way of him escaping and he would soon be dead and the information would be lost with him. Tears flooded his eyes but he was careful not to let Blackie and Antonio realize his fears.

'Pass me the vino Blackie,' Antonio laughed in an ominous blood curdling cackle. 'Now I drink, soon I kill,' he ended grabbing the Banks DIH brewed wine from Blackie.

Eddie thought Blackie's shuddering at the sight of cruelty of Antonio showed only one of these killers was humane.

Antonio laughed again and added in a crude philosophical way, 'They say that man is an animal, so you see amigo, I don't kill men, I kill animals.'

Eddie's strength was ebbing fast. He just managed to keep himself from falling into unconsciousness. He kept repeating quietly under his breath, 'don't sleep, stay awake, keep your eyes open.'

The silence was broken when Antonio informed Blackie that he would not kill Eddie. Eddie heard this and felt a little sense of relief and hope, but this glimmer of hope dissipated when Antonio said, 'I know of a better way for him to die.'

'You'll leave him here to starve to death?' asked Blackie.

'Si amigo, but he will die under better circumstances,' said the cruel mercenary. 'We'll tie him to this chair, put a noose around his neck then put the chair onto this box, with the hombre inside of course, after that we tie the loose end of the rope to the roof. Then if he tries to escape, the chair falls off the box and the little hombre dies by hanging, what you say Blackie?'

'I say you're a confounded beast, the first opportunity I get I'll shoot you.'

'It'll be a good way to die amigo, I saw a hombre die like that in Africa when I was fighting there. If you don't want him to die like that, then you kill him yourself!' said the scheming Antonio as he raised the bottle and took a few gulps.

'Do it your way,' the horrified Blackie bellowed. 'I'm no murderer.'

'Just as I thought, Blackie, a little more vino and then I'll have you in a good position amigo.'

A short time later, Eddie was hovering between life and death, precariously perched on a box with a rope around his neck. The slightest movement made and he would be an inhabitant of the other world, hanged by the neck.

'When Señor Bollers comes, we'll be gone amigo,' Antonio said. 'By the way amigo, if you breathe too hard, or if a butterfly touches you, you're gone.'

Eddie sat motionless hoping against fate that the tables would be turned on such ruthless men.

TRAILING A SUSPECT

'Come in James, are you reading me?' asked Henry, over the radio.

'Loud and clear pal, have you sighted anything?'

'Nothing yet, anything your way?'

'Quite a lot. I am parked in front of Stabroek Market enjoying a glass of mauby and a pourie, where are you?'

'At the back of Festival City, no luck this way, I'm heading back to town,'

'I'll stay here,' James informed him

'Okay, I'll be there in about ten minutes, I will drive along Homestretch Avenue.'

'Traffic shouldn't be too congested at this time.'

'Okay, there's a telephone booth across the road opposite Demico House, I'll give the girls a call, all for now, call me when you get to Brickdam.'

James got to the telephone but had to wait a few minutes because someone was in the booth making a call. He wondered when technology would get to the stage where everyone will have their own device capable of making calls from anywhere they wanted. As he thought about it, he had to admit that the idea may just be possible in his lifetime.

When the telephone booth was empty, he made the call directly to Abiola's room.

'Hello, Abi,' began James.

'Have you found him, have you found Eddie?' Abiola blurted out.

'Hold on Abi, relax. I'll bring you up to date about everything.'

'Oh James we can't take it, go on, please go on please,' she begged.

Shelly and Anita huddled around Abiola as they awaited information about Eddie. James explained to the anxious and dejected girls that there was still no trace of Eddie, but Supt. Clarke was taking a personal interest in the case and had assigned about a few detectives to help with the investigation.

'What's happening at your end?'

'Nothing much, students just hurrying around preparing for the closing party tonight,' she explained with obvious sadness and dejection in her voice.

'I know, Abi.'

'It's a pity but it seems that we will have to miss that party tonight.'

'Appears so, and to think that we planned for the last few months, but as Aunt May, the village ground provision vendor would say, man appoints but God disappoints. By the way, have you seen Denny Bollers?'

'Yes, he left about two hours ago, special taxi called for him.'

'Wonder where he gets all that money to spend around,' James asked rhetorically. 'I have a suspicion that he knows much more than he is admitting and that he is deeply involved in this.'

'Just as Anita was surmising.'

'Please tell Mr. Sam that we are still scouting for signs and clues about Eddie,' James told her. 'Henry is on his way here, he checked the South Ruimveldt and Festival City Areas. He may have even searched around Sophia where they are building the new housing scheme.'

'Okay I will do all that you ask and bring Shelly and Anita up to date. They are leaning all over me trying to hear you,' Abiola said.

'Fine, and thanks. Remember to keep everything close to your heart for the moment. Wait, hold a minute Abi, I have just spotted Bollers hurrying towards the East Bank car park, I think that I will follow him. Bye, will call you later,' he told her and ran from the telephone booth.

James followed at a safe distance. Bollers spoke to a few taxi drivers. He was trying to get a taxi of course. James thought about his car, but couldn't let Bollers out of his sight. He ran to the old man nearby. 'Old timer, watch that man in the blue shirt for a dollar, I'll be back in a minute.'

'Sorry son. I'm willing but blind in both eyes,' replied the old man.

'You want that man shadowed you mean?' asked a teenager selling a bundle of Evening Post newspapers.

'Yes,' said James.

'Cost you five dollars to watch him and five more to tell you about him,' said the newspaper boy.

'It's a deal,' said James, as he raced to his parked car.

A police officer confronted him, 'Is this your car young man?'

'Sure officer, this is my ride,' answered James as he pulled the door open and prepared to turn on the ignition.

'This is a no parking zone. Sorry, but you can't leave now,' said the traffic police officer sternly.

Valuable time was being wasted, 'I'm after a suspect,' James informed him.

He whipped out his identification card from his wallet and gave it to the police officer. 'Can't explain now, just take that to police headquarters and ask to speak to Supt. Clarke relate what happened and also let him know that I may be heading up the East Bank,' the young sleuth said as he turned the ignition on and put the car into gear.

Before the officer could regain his composure, James was winding his way towards where he had left the newspaper boy as a lookout. 'Where is he, which way did he go?' he asked anxiously. There was a singularity and purpose of mind that Bollers was someway involved in Eddie's disappearance and he had to find out what it was.

'Money before information,' was the boy's reply in between his shout to 'get your Evening Post here!'

'Here's the ten dollars, and don't keep me waiting,' James said impatiently.

'He's in that black Morris Oxford up ahead,' said the youngster pocketing the money.

James cautiously maneuvered two cars behind the Morris Oxford that was heading out of town.

When the traffic eased around Agricola he pulled his cap on and donned a pair of sunglasses as a disguise. To further ensure that Bollers did not recognize him, he tucked a tobacco less pipe into his mouth. He kept the car at a safe distance behind the Black Morris Oxford and called Henry on the radio, 'Hello Henry, where are you?'

'Lurking around the market square looking for you or signs of the car,' Henry answered.

'You wouldn't find me there, I'm heading for Timehri, trailing Bollers he seems to be in a great hurry to get there, I intend trailing him to find out exactly what he is up to.'

'How far are you?'.

'Just approaching the Linden—Soesdyke Highway,' James informed him and traveling at a moderate 97 kph. 'You know these cops patrolling the Highway always handing out speeding tickets.'

'I know that all right even when you are well below the speed limit.'

'Yea, that's how they make their side pay, threatening to give you a $100.00 speeding ticket which they know you are in no position to pay,' James elaborated.

'Indeed, then you offer them $20.00 or $30.00 and they give you a warning and send you on your way,' said Henry with a wry giggle since he had done that on a number of occasions.

It was a well-known fact that police officers had mastered the art of bribe taking at traffic training school although it was not a part of their curriculum. They discussed among themselves various strategies such as passing the hand to collect the bribe, the correct turning of the body to obscure the public gaze and folding the money into fake traffic tickets.

The taxi drivers and ordinary motorists have also devised and mastered their own methods of passing on the bribes. 'You're traveling at 97 kph, I'll be going a lot faster. Mr. Sam's car has a siren a privilege for being a Major in the volunteer army, The People's

Militia, I'm sure if I activate it your uncle will understand,' said Henry.

'Take it easy Henry, not too much speed,' cautioned James.

'Sure pal, I'll cruise at about seventy or eighty.'

With siren blaring and traffic at a standstill to allow him to pass through unhindered, Henry sped after James and Bollers.

Twenty minutes later James radioed Henry. 'We're almost there, just passing the army barracks,' James told him. 'The taxi is moving dangerously fast.'

'I'm about ten minutes behind you; I'll step on the gas.'

'It's okay to do so now; there is virtually no traffic.'

Still in disguise, James pulled up at the taxi port about 30 meters to the left of Bollers' taxi. Bollers hurried out and hastily flipped a bill, probably a Malali to the taxi driver. Without waiting to collect his change, he hurried towards the departure lounge.

James radioed Henry, 'Bollers has exited the taxi and is heading towards the departure lounge over and out.' He then parked his car and rushed to the taxi driver who was preparing to depart the airport. 'Five dollars to tell the driver of a white Jagan Lotus due here in about two minutes to wait for me at my car over there,' he shouted.

'Wait a minute, are you guys crazy, just throwing away money? That guy just overpaid me five times my fare and did not collect his change, now you are giving me five dollars for a favour?' he said in amazement. 'When it rains it pours.'

'Please do as I say, I'm in a hurry,' he begged, as he discarded his improvised disguise and tucked the empty pipe into his back pocket. He elbowed his way through the crowd to keep Bollers in sight. Bollers stopped a Custom's Officer and spoke with a clerk. She listened then summoned a uniformed guard. The guard spoke with Bollers then ushered him behind a door marked 'No unauthorized Entry.'

James rushed to the clerk that Bollers had spoken to. 'It seems,' he said feigning great concern and hurry, 'I am afraid that I have just missed my friend.'

'Who is he?' she asked airily.

'The one who was escorted by the guard into that room,' he said panting. 'I saw him late, I couldn't shout, it would have been very unmannerly.'

'I see, Mr. Warren,' she began.

'Not the guard,' James said. 'The other younger guy.'

'The young man, Mr. Alphonso Warren, isn't he your friend? You said he was,' the charming girl said. 'You should at least know his name.'

'Sorry ma'am I was excited, I wasn't even concentrating on what you were saying,' said James feeling very embarrassed.

James was absolutely sure that he was on to something.

'When is his flight scheduled to depart?' he asked. 'You see it's important, I must see him before he leaves,' lied James.

'He's on a private flight,' she said. 'I'm sorry.'

'It's important,' he pleaded looking deeply forlorn and abjectly disappointed.

'Hold on. Let me check that out for you,' she said as she picked up the telephone and dialed.

'He's scheduled to leave in ten minutes,' she told him.

'I know it's too much to ask, but can you help me on the runway?' he asked in a tone underlining urgency.

'This is unauthorized, but I have a brother who is an airplane mechanic, he may be able to help, hold on a second,' she said.

'I'll be right back and please check the registration number of the aircraft for me,' he said as he hurried to rendezvous with Henry.

He found Henry with a pensive look on his face standing between the cars. 'Hurry Henry! No time to explain now, we're on to something tangible!'

Henry hurried after James. Forgetting courtesy, they hastily wound their way to the helpful clerk.

'This is my brother, Keith, he'll help you through the security. Unusual precautions but it seems as though something strange is happening. The aircraft's number is BXL 804 TR. Is that important to you?' she asked.

'Sure it's very important and thank you,' James said, as he urged Keith on.

At the gateway, they were confronted by armed soldiers and other security men. 'Buddies of mine,' said Keith as he produced his security pass and guided them through.

'There he is,' said Henry pointing to a hurrying figure in the distance.

A blue and red aircraft taxied along the runway and halted about fifty meters from Bollers. He glanced at his watch and then backwards as he walked energetically towards the aircraft. 'If he gets into that we'll lose him for sure,' James said.

'You guys are under my care, just keep out of harm's way. I would be over there by that helicopter, the pilot's my friend,' Keith said.

'You bet we will,' Henry assured him as they shortened their strides, 'but it may be better if we accompany you.'

'Know the owner of that kite?' Henry asked.

'No,' Keith answered as they walked towards the helicopter.

A door opened at the side of the fuselage and a rope ladder was thrown out. Bollers ascended the ladder and was obscured from view. 'What rotten luck!' exclaimed James in utter bewilderment. 'After all this fatigue and now he has escaped. In a few minutes we'll be watching him soar out of sight and disappear,' he said, more in soliloquy. Keith meanwhile had decided that the civilians were walking too slowly and had lengthened his stride.

'Why don't we inform the authorities that Bollers is a crook?' suggested Henry.

'Who'd believe us? Not even our fathers and some people may even say that because we're educated we are making fools out of them,' said James. 'What can we do now?' he murmured to himself.

'Let's steal a plane and follow him then hope that it pays dividends,' said Henry jokingly.

'Yea, who'll fly it anyway, we can't even fly kites on Easter Monday, much less airplanes?' teased James, still finding room for some humor amidst the dire situation. Keith by this time had reached the helicopter and was talking to the pilot.

'Then I suggest that we contact Keith, let him help us locate where the aircraft is bound and the approximate time of arrival,' Henry suggested.

'Excellent idea,' James concurred, 'then we can have Uncle Patrick contact the Army Air Force wing.'

James started at a fast run towards the helicopter. Henry followed at an equal pace. They found Keith chatting with the pilot. 'These are the two boys I was telling you about Ernest. Forgive me, but I don't even know their names, they were in such a hurry to catch that man,' he explained.

'I'm James and this is Henry. Sorry that we didn't meet under better circumstances we are amateur detectives and were on the trail of a suspect until he entered that plane.'

'Sorry to hear that you have lost him, I am Keith Whyte and this is the pilot, Captain Ernest Persaud one of the most skillful pilots we have in Guyana,' Keith elaborated with a broad smile.

The boys were stunned. They stared at the militarily clad figure unbelievably. Both Keith and Captain Persaud were taken aback and equally amazed.

'Are you Captain Persaud?' they chorused.

'Yes, I am Captain Persaud of course, why?' he asked looking at the boys intently and with cautious optimism.

'Is the registration number of this helicopter XRG 58 HT?' Henry asked eagerly, a twinkle appearing in his eyes.

'That's exactly right, but how did you know that?' asked the captain.

'We got it from Mr. Cheong,' began James.

'Mr. Cheong, the famous archeologist? Which one of you is Clarke?'

They were distracted momentarily by the revving motors of the plane.

'I am Clarke, James Clarke!'

'Did you say a suspect is on that plane? It seems as though my vacation is over,' Captain Persaud added as he yanked the door of the helicopter open.

The boys' eyes widened with amazement at the sudden turn of events. Keith Whyte admitted in a barely audible monotone. 'I don't understand. It's beyond my comprehension.'

'Hop in guys and put these on. Care to come with us Keith? We may need your help in case we run into trouble. I will radio your boss at the airport and also headquarters.'

'Yes I sure will.'

They put on the headsets and watched as the blue and red airplane taxied along the runway. It then turned slowly awaiting the signaler's flags. Meanwhile Captain Persaud did his checks and informed the control tower that he had the advantage of a vertical take-off. After a few seconds, Captain Persaud pushed the right joy stick forward and balanced the right and left, ascended and hovered twenty meters above the runway. The plane shot off the runway and rose majestically into the blue Demerara skies. Captain Persaud made a banked turn and at a safe altitude below the plane shot followed at a discreet distance.

'Wouldn't the other pilot become suspicious when he spots us following?' asked James and the captain informed them that it was not unusual for aircrafts to travel very long distances following each other especially when going to the interior.

Once airborne the boys began to fill in Captain Persaud and Keith with the details and he in turn indicated that Mr. Cheong was a friend and that they had worked excavating archeological sites at places such as Aishalton, Kurupung and the mountainous areas of the Kanuku ranges deep in Macushi settlements.

'He radioed me some time ago and told of unearthing massive amounts of valuables like gold, diamonds and other artifacts, turtle shells and ornaments, fish boned tip arrows and spears that could be at least 2,000 years old. He also indicated that he was sure of making bigger discoveries then suddenly, he started receiving death threats coupled with unusual accidents and even more sinister activities around the area,' Captain Persaud told the boys. 'He also mentioned something about Clarke and that his help would be solicited in solving the puzzling mysteries.'

Captain Persaud radioed Timehri Airport for information about the plane and obtained the flight route, destination and time of arrival. The plane was scheduled to arrive at Orinduik later in the afternoon. He also informed them of Keith's absence.

'Can't trail them to Orinduik I only have fuel for two hours of flying,' he said.

'What luck!' exclaimed Henry, 'Eddie may be in grave danger by now, I'm sure that the plane is leading us to the gang's hideout.'

Captain Persaud then radioed the army and police headquarters. Supt. Clarke reported they had no information as to the whereabouts of Eddie James. The helicopter flew at a lower altitude and approximately a mile behind the airplane which Captain Persaud pointed out was moving unusually slow. The helicopter made occasional circles and dives to divert attention.

'Seems that we have to turn back, those guys up ahead are right on course and heading for Orinduik. Here we go back to Timehri,' said the dejected pilot, as he steadied the helicopter skillfully then turned gracefully.

Henry and James lost all hope of finding their pal.

SAVING EDDIE

'Hey, wait a second! That plane has just gone off course' said Captain Persaud. 'It seems to be heading to Linden. Here we go again, hold tight!' he said, as he banked the helicopter in pursuit.

James was in the co-pilot's seat and Henry and their newly found friend, Keith behind. 'This will be tricky captain, we want to know what those guys are up to.'

'Sure thing,' Henry quipped in, 'I think they are going to see how Eddie's getting along, somehow I'm positive they know something about his whereabouts.'

'Anyway, captain, radio police headquarters and tell Supt. Clarke of the new developments,' James suggested and Captain Persaud agreed.

'I think they are nearing their destination,' said the pilot. 'Those flashing lights are landing signals.'

'Where are they, captain?' James asked.

'Along the highway in the vicinity of Loo Creek. Probably they have a hide-out there, perfect place for a hideout you know, numerous forested areas and good compressed sand for a landing strip.'

'But wouldn't they see us?' asked Keith.

'Not unless they turn, the pilot's attention is now undivided. He's concentrating on a safe landing,' said the experienced pilot.

'What if we land here, captain? After all, that plane may be equipped with guns?' said Henry.

'Yes, we can land here, and when they leave we take a peek at the landing strip,' said James.

'If that's the way you want it,' said the captain as he brought the helicopter to a smooth landing on a fifty foot clearing.

With engines cut, they listened and heard the purr of the airplane clearly through the woods. Keith estimated the landing strip to be about a kilometer off. They hadn't a long wait because five minutes later the blue and red aircraft streaked past.

'Finished what they had to do real quick,' said Henry.

'Yeah, I guess they just had to pick up or drop off a skunk or two and move,' said James.

'Do you think they saw us?' asked Henry.

'Not on your life,' answered Captain Persaud. 'The trees acted as a perfect camouflage for the helicopter.

Just as the airplane was out of sight they were again airborne and this time heading for the area where the plane had landed minutes before.

'This is it,' said Captain Persaud, as he skimmed the top of the trees. 'Here we go, that's the strip ahead.'

They landed and quickly got out of the helicopter.

'Let's look for foot prints and follow them. They may lead us somewhere,' said James.

'Here are two sets of prints,' Captain Persaud announced, 'from the distance between them, it seems as though the two persons sprinted to the plane when it landed.'

Captain Persaud drew his pistol and they set out in single file following the footprints. The prints were clearly visible in the white sand. They led the group away from the clearing into the wooded hills. The sun was setting and its crimson glow that offered some luminosity was soon obscured by the overhanging trees and shrubs. The vegetation in this particular area was abundant and many small entrepreneurs would participate in wood burning to produce charcoal.

'Can't see a darn thing,' said Captain Persaud.

'We'll need torchlight,' said James.

'I have one in the helicopter,' said the captain.

Keith and Henry rushed back to fetch the torchlight and James and the captain eagerly awaited their return. When they did return they resumed their quest.

'Can't say if we are on the right track,' said Henry.

'Keep going,' James said, suddenly he stopped. 'Here are a few scattered dry leaves, seemed as though they were just upturned.' They slowly wormed their way through the trees.

'Look a hut!' shouted Henry excitedly. 'Sure looks to me like one used by the charcoal makers.'

Up ahead and secretly behind a clump of trees was a small hut with a thatched roof.

'Careful,' cautioned James. 'We should surround it, since if there's anyone inside they'll be armed.'

They sneaked up to the four sides of the hut. Captain Persaud with his gun, rushed towards the door and heaved his shoulders against the old structure, but it was opened. The others joined him. They entered quietly, James flicked the torchlight on.

'My God!' they exclaimed as their eyes met the horrible sight of Eddie, eyes half open, clinging desperately to life and perched on a box with a rope around his neck.

James gripped the weak crumble form and steadied the chair, as Henry fumbled with the tangled noose around his neck. Captain Persaud and Keith assisted the two in lowering Eddie on to the cold floor. He half opened his eyes and feigned a smile. Seconds later he lapsed into unconsciousness.

'We'll have to hurry,' James urged. 'Any delay can prove fatal.'

The helicopter landed at army headquarters, Thomas Lands, and the army ambulance whisked the unconscious Eddie to the Georgetown Hospital. Three army security officers accompanied Henry, James and Keith to the Hospital where Eddie was immediately taken to the emergency room. Time literally stood still, as the boys waited for word about Eddie's condition. Captain Persaud and another Lieutenant arrived thirty minutes later with four armed soldiers who took up positions outside the emergency room.

'We'll escort you back to headquarters, when your friend has been taken care of,' said the Lieutenant. 'Have you heard anything yet?'

'Nothing,' James answered.

Just then a door opened and a doctor approached them with measured steps.

'He'll be all right,' the doctor informed them, 'all that he'll need is a long rest probably three or four days and lots of fluids since he's dehydrated, and good nourishment.'

James and Henry sighed with relief; a great weight had been taken off their shoulders.

'Thank you, doctor,' said James extending his hands. 'I am James Clarke, and this is Keith Whyte and my friend Henry Major.'

'Glad to have met you, I am Major Leyland Heyliger,' he said.

The boys seemed a bit flabbergasted that there were so many military personnel around and Henry asked the reason.

'I cannot give the reason, maybe my superior officer could but yes,' answered Captain Persaud who was conversing with the Lieutenant, 'the porters who brought your friend in, the nurses who will be helping with his care and recuperation and the doctors who examined him are all military personnel,' he further explained.

'Is there any particular reason?' asked Henry, directing his question to the Major.

'Well you see, this is under the strictest security because we suspect that it is linked in some way to a perceived military coup and even an outbreak of war,' Major Heyliger said.

The boys were pop eyed at this disclosure and they were so stunned and dumbfounded at this revelation that they couldn't ask a further question. The Major continued unabashed, 'Your friend Keith here is also an army security officer.'

'Sorry to have you so baffled, but you are detectives you will understand, my sister you spoke to at the airport is an intelligence officer, Sergeant Bernice Whyte. She didn't trust you so she called me in to keep an eye on you. Hope that you will forgive her, but in such cases you can't trust anyone, not even yourself at times.'

There were so many questions that James and Henry wanted to ask, but they just couldn't. All the information they had just received was too much for them to process and much of it was top national secret.

'We have been working on this case for some time now,' said the young Lieutenant, 'but didn't make any substantial progress until you boys showed up,' he informed them. 'We'll take you back with us to army headquarters. Your friend Eddie is now in safe hands and will get all the expert care he needs to recuperate.'

They returned to Camp Ayangana approximately seven hours after the ordeal began.

'I guess you guys are hungry and starving,' said Lieutenant Heyliger.

'Sure right about that,' chirped Henry.

'Fine, we are on our way to the officers eating quarters. You'll be taken care of.'

'Can I make some phone calls before I settle down to meals?' asked James.

'Sure, just across in the guard room. Please accompany him, Sergeant Whyte,' said the Major.

Keith and James hurried over to the guard hut to make the calls as the others continued to the officers dining quarters. When Keith and James got to the telephone, it was occupied by a well-dressed lower rank who immediately hung up the telephone when the Sergeant arrived. Keith politely asked him for some privacy and left James to make his calls. He and the Private stepped outside the guard hut and began a conversation about cricket and the exploits of Clive Lloyd and Roy Fredericks, two of a long line of Guyanese cricketers who represented the West Indies. Other notables included Rohan Kanhai, Basil Butcher, Alvin Kalicharran, Steve Camacho, Lance Gibbs and Joe Solomon. James hoped that he would remember to tune in to The Guyana Broadcasting Service (GBS) later that night to catch the legendary BL Crombie on his sports cast.

James realized it was late afternoon and decided he should call the Turkeyen campus to give Abiola an update. 'May I speak to Abiola Clarke?' he asked politely. 'This is her cousin James.'

The receptionist recognized the voice immediately and informed him that the girls, Abiola, Anita and Shelly were in a meeting with the Principal, Mr. Sam.

'Please hold on a minute,' she said and walked to Mr. Sam's door and knocked timidly. She was recently employed at the college and as new employees always do, she was calm and respectful until she learned the ropes, then she could be a part of the workplace culture and act accordingly.

Abiola exited Mr. Sam's office and retrieved the telephone from the receptionist's desk. 'Hello, this is Abiola speaking', she said excitedly. Evidently, the receptionist had informed the group that James was the caller.

'Hi Abi,' James greeted her with reciprocal excitement. 'Everything is fine. We found Eddie. Have the receptionist transfer the call to Mr. Sam's office so that we can be on speaker phone,' James said.

The call was transferred to Mr. Sam's office where they could all listen and speak as a group. 'Thank heavens! Eddie is safe, we were all so worried and dejected. The pain and worry was overwhelming. Anita really took it hard. She hasn't eaten anything since breakfast.'

'Where are you now?' Mr. Sam asked, showing a calmness that he hadn't exhibited for many hours. The profuse sweating had definitely eased and the wavering in his voice had subsided. There was no fidgeting for cigars or handkerchiefs; he was back to his normal self. A huge weight had been taken off his shoulders.

'I am at army headquarters with Henry in the distinguished company of top army brass. Eddie is at the Georgetown Hospital under special armed guard,' James informed them. 'Tell Anita that Eddie is okay and not to worry. She must relax,' he reassured her.

After instilling the need for secrecy, James promised that he and Henry would be returning to the college soon. James then placed a call to his uncle at the police headquarters. 'Supt. Clarke, please,' he said.

'The superintendent is in a very important meeting with the commissioner of police at present,' was the terse reply.

'What about his Special Assistant Inspector Jordan?' James asked.

'I am sorry, he's attending the meeting also,' came the reply.

'This is of grave importance. Please inform him that there is an important call from James Clarke and don't be worried or afraid to interrupt the meeting. You will not be reprimanded or demoted. You may even be promoted,' James said with an air of confidence.

The officer at the other end debated a few seconds then reluctantly shrugged his shoulder walked to the closed door of the Commissioner's office, tapped gently and delivered the message from James.

The Commissioner thanked him returned the salute and asked for the call to be transferred to his office. The non-commissioned officer returned, saluted and informed Supt. Clarke that James was on the telephone. A second later, Supt. Clarke was speaking animatedly with his nephew. 'Where are you, James?' he asked.

'At army headquarters. Everything is fine. We found Eddie in a hut at Loo Creek off the Linden Soesdyke Highway. The army is working on a case also for all I know, the two cases may be linked in some way.'

James gave him some minor details about Eddie's injuries and overall physical condition. He listened, then informed him that he shouldn't be surprised if he sees them at army headquarters.

'That's all for now uncle, here's hoping that you do make it. Bye, see you later,' he said as he hung up the telephone.

He and Keith walked back to the dining area where they washed up and joined the others. They ate and talked ordinarily. Henry commented on the fine cuisine and particularly about the curry roti and chowmein. As an added treat the cooks had prepared conkee wrapped in banana leaves.

'Wonder what Eddie would say when he learns about the mini feast he missed here,' said Henry as he sipped a glass of warm cow's milk and chewed on conkee.

'Guess he'll want to join the army,' said James.

They all laughed when they learnt that Eddie's hobby was eating and his first love his belly. James then informed them that Supt. Clarke, Inspector Jordan and the Police Commissioner may be at headquarters later. After the hearty meal they were led by Captain Persaud to the Base Commander's office and were pleasantly surprised that the three police officers were already there. After introductions and salutes, the Commander Brigadier Hawley Gillis invited Henry and James to give the gathering a detailed account of the mystery and the kidnapping of Eddie. James told of the petroglyphs found with the broken glass shade, the stolen letter and the car that tried to run them down. Henry then took over and told of the night prowler and the mysterious message sent by Mr. Cheong and its link to Captain Persaud. James again took up the narrative telling the attentive group of Eddie's disappearance, the chase to the Timehri airport and locating Eddie.

As James mentioned Timehri Airport he wondered when Guyana would follow the trend of naming their international ports of entry after famous citizens and political leaders. There's the Norman Manley International in Jamaica, Errol Barrow in Barbados. He smiled as he considered some possible names. Linden Burnham International? No, that would be unfair he already has a city named after him, the bauxite mining town of Linden. Maybe our first President Arthur Chung and what about Cheddi Jagan International? He has done a lot for Guyana and who knows, he may one day become our first Indian President?

'You boys have done a fantastic job so far, but there is much more to do,' said Supt. Clarke.

'Marvelous indeed, I am proud of all of you. What did you say the registration number of that aircraft was? We can check it out with the authorities,' Brigadier Gillis said.

Without hesitation James repeated the number, 'It's BXL 804 TR.'

'Sergeant Whyte, check every detail about that aircraft, registration and ownership. Then report back immediately,' the Brigadier said.

Keith saluted his superior officer as customary, made an about turn and left. 'What do you think Superintendent?' asked Brigadier Gillis.

'I think that we are up against a stronger, more organized and ruthless gang than we ever suspected,' was the pained but honest reply from Supt. Clarke.

'It does appear so,' agreed the Commander. 'From some of the radio transmissions we have intercepted it seems as though there is something building up around the Essequibo Region. There have also been numerous cross border incursions from our western neighbour,' he further explained.

The group listened intently. No one was asking any questions but only shaking their heads in disbelief. The Commander continued unabashed. 'These incursions have been made by civilian boats, helicopters and airplanes, not any military crafts,' he explained. 'Although we have dispatched additional personnel, equipment and troops, we have been unable to find any tangible proof of drug smuggling, contraband running or any other nefarious activities,' the Commander said with a frustrated look.

'Then there have been threats on Mr. Cheong's life,' Captain Persaud interjected. 'He reported that all his scientific reports and detailed evacuations drawings have been stolen and unusual blasts have caused many of his dedicated native Amerindian workers to desert him,' Captain Persaud further elaborated.

They listened as Captain Persaud talked about the hardships being endured by Mr. Cheong in the unforgiving interior and the harsh mountainous terrain of the Kanuku. Mr. Cheong has also said that he will conclude all excavations in that region and return to Georgetown in three days.

'When did you get the message, Captain Persaud?' James asked thoughtfully.

'Two days ago.'

'My goodness!' James exclaimed. 'Then he should be departing for Georgetown tomorrow. Can a message be sent to him to hold on a little longer?'

'Why?' asked Inspector Jordan who had looked contemplative during the discussions.

'The only logical explanation to this is that Mr. Cheong is operating within the sphere of this gang and they want him out of the way so that they could carry out their activities unhindered and undisturbed. As for the antiques discovered, they fetch valuable prices abroad. I believe that they are stolen, smuggled out of the country and sold to foreign dealers,' James said.

'So you believe they are stolen, shipped out of the country and sold on the black market!' said the Lieutenant.

'Exactly,' answered James, 'the money obtained is used to finance whatever activities are taking place in the area.'

'I believe you may be along the correct lines,' said the Commander, 'Captain Persaud, radio Mr. Cheong immediately, tell him to stay put, we are sending reinforcements. Lieutenant, get twelve volunteers from the Special Forces unit, they will be flown out tonight to assist Mr. Cheong. They'll parade as civilians to avoid suspicion, arrange a special briefing for 21:00 hours.'

'I'll send along one of our best detectives, Inspector Steve Williams,' said Supt. Clarke. 'This is of national importance, so it should be tackled cooperatively.'

Captain Persaud and Lieutenant James excused themselves from the group. 'There may be a new twist to this affair when we learn who Eddie was following and who kept him in that secluded hut,' said Henry.

'That's right,' admitted Brigadier Gillis. 'By tomorrow afternoon he may be fit for interrogation. What if we visit him at five o'clock?'

They all agreed. Half an hour later, the gathering was back to its original strength with the return of Sergeant Keith Whyte, Lieutenant James and Captain Persaud. Lieutenant James said that he had obtained the volunteers and that they were eager to know about the mission. The captain also said that a section of Mr. Cheong's recent excavations had been booby-trapped and blown to smithereens. Two guards at the site were wounded and had to be flown to Georgetown. The rest of the workers have all abandoned their posts and have arranged with the pilot of a blue and red plane to be flown out this evening.

James responded immediately with a surprised look. 'A red and blue plane?' he asked.

'Yes, that's what Mr. Cheong said,' answered the captain, 'a six seater.'

'But, captain, could it be the same plane that we trailed to Loo Creek?' asked James.

The others were astonished at the flow of events and the linkages made by James. 'Why fly to Georgetown?' asked Henry.

'By taking the workers, he ensures that Mr. Cheong's work would be brought to a standstill and he'll eventually have to leave. They will then be able to operate unencumbered and without fear of disturbances and intruders.'

'Seems logical,' they all admitted.

'Then, I doubt the plane would be flying to Georgetown.'

'Why not?' asked Supt. Clarke.

'Before I answer Uncle Patrick, captain, how many workers are flying out? Did Mr. Cheong say?' James asked.

'Yes, Mr. Cheong clearly said all ten of his workers.'

'Fine, you said the plane is a six-seater, but with ten workers and the pilot that would be eleven and I doubt that any pilot in his right frame of mind, would over load a plane,' said James. 'It constitutes a serious breach of flying regulations.'

'The boy's right,' admitted Captain Persaud. 'That's about the first thing they tell you at flying school.'

'So, if he doesn't fly to Georgetown, what will he do?' asked James

Keith who had been tasked by Brigadier Gillis to get all details about the aircraft said, 'Circle and land in the same area then recruit the workers to whatever business they are engaged in. The pilot of the plane is an antique dealer named Gus Carrington. He usually has a Frenchman named Rene Francois, one of his workers, to conduct his affairs while he's away. He lived in Bel Air Gardens until two days ago when he posted a 'FOR RENT' sign on the front fence,' Keith informed them.

'Where does he live now?' asked Supt. Clarke.

'That seems a mystery to the authorities,' answered Keith. 'He just disappeared, dropped out of sight.'

'So, that puts two more suspects on the list, Gus Carrington and Rene Durant, in addition to Bollers, Walcott, Blackie and Antonio,' said Henry.

They called the meeting closed a short time later with a reminder to meet at the hospital the following afternoon. James invited Keith to the closing party and also extended through him an invitation to his helpful sister, the airport clerk. Captain Persaud was unable to accept because of the pressure of work. He nevertheless offered to take the boys to Turkeyen in the helicopter because their cars were left at the airport.

After goodbyes and salutes, Henry and James once again boarded the helicopter, this time heading for the college campus. They landed shortly before dark. Students flocked the lawns not knowing who the dignitary was. Jack and Robert admitted later that they thought it was the Prime Minister or Cicely Baird, the Minister of Education. James and Henry stepped off the helicopter, bending below the rotating blades to the amazement of the large gathering. They cleared the whirring blades and were quickly joined by Shelly, Anita and Abiola. They made their way through the inquiring mob towards Mr. Sam's residence.

They brought Mr. Sam and the girls up to date, filling in as concisely as they could the details of the day's proceedings, including Eddie's condition and their meeting at the army headquarters. They also told of their invitation to Keith Whyte and his sister Bernice. Both Henry and James were extremely tired, so they excused themselves, wished Mr. Sam a pleasant night's rest, and escorted the girls back to their dormitory. They then retired to their own quarters for a short rest before preparing for the party.

THE CAPTURE OF ALFIE WALCOTT

James and Henry woke late that morning suffering from the after effects of the party. Although they were not regular drinkers, they got away from the girls under the pretense of using the bathroom. They took Keith to Shaboo's corner shop and treated themselves to a cold Banks beer to celebrate their new found friendship with Keith. A toast was also offered to Eddie's health and speedy recovery.

'I feel like a bag of sugar,' said James, 'heavy and awkward.'

'It was a grand evening.'

'Yes, I enjoyed every moment of it. If only Eddie were here,' James lamented.

'Sure missed him. I wonder how he spent the night.'

'When this case is over, we'll have a special get together and we'll be sure to invite Keith and Bernice over.'

'Yea, Bernice is a real marvel,' admitted Henry. 'She's cute and moves like a butterfly when she's dancing.'

'Oh! I nearly forgot, we have to collect the cars from the airport. What if we collect the girls and take them along?'

'Good idea, they'll love that.'

'I'm not sure about Anita, she kept repeating last night that she'll be visiting the hospital first thing in the morning.'

'With the strict security and his condition, I doubt whether she will get the opportunity to see him.'

They dressed, had breakfast, and then visited the girls.

'Thought you were still sleeping,' teased James.

'Not on your life! We were up very early. Don't you realize that we're expected to leave the dormitory by this afternoon?' said Shelly.

'Oh jeeps! We forgot. Haven't even started packing,' said Henry.

'Good for you. We are finished and ready to go,' said Abiola. 'We are spending a week with Anita in South Ruimveldt until Eddie has recuperated fully.'

'Wow, excellent, marvelous!' exclaimed Henry. 'That would mean we wouldn't be separated for another week.'

'We have a surprise for you girls,' said James.

'Let's hear it,' they chorused.

'We want you to go with us to Timehri to collect the cars,' Henry announced.

Anita was the first to answer, 'I'm afraid I can't possibly make that trip, I want to visit Eddie,' she said earnestly and a bit teary eyed.

'Anita you wouldn't get to see him. The security, and then the doctor said absolutely no visitors,' Henry told her.

'But, Henry don't you realize I must see him,' she pleaded.

'Listen to what we'll do,' reasoned James. 'You go to the Hospital and the four of us will go to Timehri, but we'll return to Campus and take you all to South Ruimveldt.'

They agreed and soon left. Anita accompanied the four to the East Bank Car Park where they caught a taxi to Timehri. She then hurried across to the Stabroek Market Square where she purchased fruits for her sick sweetheart.

The four reached the Airport forty-five minutes later and to their amazement found an armed guard standing between the two cars.

They approached him cautiously.

'Are you the owners of these cars?' he asked.

'Have they been tampered with?' asked Henry.

'No, nothing of that sort. Last night I received orders to guard these babies until the owners arrived,' he said. 'I've been here since last evening.'

They thanked him, then hurried to see Bernice Whyte. She greeted them warmly and a few minutes later conducted them to the staff lounge where they had a snack of Guycan cherry juice, salara and quinches. Keith joined them later and offered to take them on a tour of the newly renovated control tower. Unfortunately they had to decline the offer because of their tight schedule. Both boys promised to take up the offer after the holidays. They waved goodbye to Keith and Bernice and with Abiola accompanying Henry and Shelly riding with James, they wound their way slowly away from the airport and back to the capital.

After a few miles, James stopped the car and allowed Shelly to drive. She had recently acquired her learner's permit and was due to take the driving test. Henry also stopped and gave the wheels of Mr. Sam's Forbes Lotus to Abiola. Henry and James had left the radio sets in the cars so they left the driving to the girls and proceeded to carry on a lively conversation.

'What if we check on Eddie at the hospital before returning to campus?' Shelly suggested.

'Do you believe that Anita will still be there?' James asked.

'Not really, but knowing the way a woman thinks, she may still be hanging around the waiting room area,' Shelly said with a degree of sadness.

'Right, the idea sounds wonderful,' acknowledged James who then radioed Henry with the suggestion. 'Shelly wants us to stop by the hospital in Lamaha Street to see if Anita is still there.'

'That's okay with me and Abi,' he told him.

Just then Abiola looked into the rearview mirror, 'Isn't that face familiar?' she said as they cruised past a car with the hood raised.

'I didn't look at the person,' answered Henry.

'I'm trying my best to remember where I saw him before,' she said.

'I know where you saw him,' said Henry teasingly, 'when you looked in the mirror.'

'It's no joke Henry, I am positive that I saw him before, even though it may have been fleetingly; you know that I am very good at remembering faces.'

'Sorry, my dear,' he told her.

'I remember now!' she blurted out, 'yes that's it.' She beamed genuinely pleased with herself.

'Who is he? Where did you see him?' Henry wanted to know.

'That's the man you chased after the football match against the university,' she said emphatically and with great certainty. 'There's another man with him.'

Henry was astounded. He radioed James up ahead and informed him that Abiola was certain that she had passed Alfie Walcott and an accomplice with hood raised along the road.

Abiola stopped the car and Shelly reversed. 'We should investigate,' said James, 'but if it's Walcott and he recognizes either me or Henry he'll put up a fight and try to escape.'

'Then what shall we do?' asked Henry.

'Let the girls continue driving, we'll conceal ourselves in the rear seats. Shelly would park on the other side of the road approach him and offer to help,' James said. 'If it's Walcott and he becomes agitated and aggressive I'll surprise him and come over to help.'

After serious debate and consideration and a promise that the boys did not get themselves in any unwarranted confrontation, Abiola and Shelly agreed to the plans. The girls made U-turns and headed back to where Abiola had spotted Walcott and his companion. Abiola stopped about thirty feet from the crippled vehicle while Shelly pulled up and stepped across the road to the car with the raised hood.

'Having engine trouble?' she inquired.

'Yea, what's that to you?' the man asked in a harsh tone.

'Not a single thing, my good friend,' answered Shelly cynically. 'Just thought I'll lend a poor mechanic a helping hand. Have you never heard the Bishop of the St. George's Cathedral say doing a good deed a day takes you closer to heaven?'

The man jerked his shoulders and raised his head in obvious disdain and anger and looked at her. He was tall, muscular and well built. His shoulders partly blocked the engine. 'Call me a poor mechanic, you measly scrawny girl. How can you change faulty spark plugs without spark plug spanners, you tell me that master mechanic?' he said sarcastically.

'Simply ask the scrawny, measly, master mechanic if she may have one,' Shelly informed him.

'All right, madam haughty, do you have a spark plug spanner?' he said gruffly.

'Okay, give me the darn thing, girl,' he demanded.

'Is that the way you speak to women? You should be a bit more polite. Ask again and this time don't forget the please,' Shelly told him.

He was clearly embarrassed and furious. Courtesy and etiquette were clearly not his strong points or concerns. He was now in a position of uncertainty and was definitely conflicted and confused. Send the girl on her way or swallow his pride, be humble and get the tool to fix the car? He decided that it was better to do as he was asked, 'May I borrow your spark plug spanner please?'

'You big brutes are really unmannerly,' Shelly said as she walked across to where she had left James hidden in the back seat of the car.

When Shelly got to the car she informed James in whispers that the man wasn't Alfie Walcott. 'Pretend that you can't locate the spanner and give me a few seconds to get Henry on the radio,' James told her. James broad smile showed Shelly that he was proud of her handling of the situation. It was evident that the time they had spent together discussing mysteries and tactics had paid high dividends.

'Henry, Shelly is doing a fantastic job, when she returns to the car drive up and offer to help,' James advised and then turned the radio off.

Shelly found the tool and James told her to taunt the man a bit more, then tell him that she thought his friend Alfie Walcott would have fixed the car faster. Shelly acknowledged what James told her and walked over to deliver the tool.

The man was very animated. 'Hurry up girl, we don't have the whole darn day you know,' he said.

He grabbed the tool from Shelly and stuffed his hands into the engine and began fumbling with the distributor caps. He extracted two of the six plugs, then asked for the nearest gas station. He was clearly not from this part of the country or he would have known that the gas station was less than a quarter of a mile away at Eccles.

'Care to give me a lift there? I will pay you well,' he offered realizing his predicament.

Just then Henry and Abiola rolled up. 'I sure can,' Shelly told him, 'but I thought that your friend Alfie Walcott had gone to get the plugs,' she said.

The man was clearly taken by surprise but soon recovered his composure. 'What the hell do you know about Alfie Walcott?' he asked advancing menacingly towards Shelly. Shelly retreated as Henry blocked his way. James rushed from the car to Henry's assistance. Sizing up the situation and realizing that he was out numbered, the man attacked wildly. From the man's graceful movements, Sonny Liston would have been very proud of him.

Henry ducked under a hard over hand right and pounded a left upper cut into his mid-section. He appeared not to feel the blow and kicked James as he registered a Bruce Lee karate chop. Just then a police car burst onto the scene siren blaring. The man knew then that the game was about up. He turned to flee only to be confronted by a group of school children returning from a school rally. As many pickpockets and thieves would tell you, school children are not the friendliest of individuals you would like to meet after you commit a crime. They mob you, chase you down and prevent your escape until the police arrive.

He cursed violently as he was hemmed in by the crowd. He was then handcuffed by an officer and thrown into the back of the police van and transported to the police headquarters for questioning. James requested an armed police officer to guard Walcott's car, then followed the police officers with the suspect to police headquarters. After making written statements and voicing their opinions to the police officers, they headed for Supt. Clarke's office. Supt. Clarke was delighted when he heard that they had nabbed a suspect and of the important roles played by Abiola and Shelly.

'Good for you girls,' said Supt. Clarke, 'It's not easy being a detective, you know.'

'Uncle, we'll like to check that car for clues, I doubt whether we'll learn anything from that man,' James said.

Supt. Clarke telephoned the Eve Leary Headquarters and informed the group that the car was on its way and that the only information the man had given was his name, Tommy Harris and that he will be occupying a cell until they got more information.

A crash truck brought the car to the Brickdam Police compound where Supt. Clarke along with four detectives carried out a minute check on the vehicle. The doors and the interior were meticulously dusted for finger prints. Henry and James discovered a box in the trunk with neatly wrapped parcels and two automatic rifles. The parcels were addressed to dealers in France, America and England and the contents were carvings, pieces of sculpture, beads, bone arrow heads and rock tools. The curator of the National Museum later identified the articles as ancient Amerindian artifacts and craft of the fourth century and further ascribed the collection to having originated around the Dawana area. A similar scrap of paper as the one that was found with the broken shade was also found in an envelope addressed to Alfie Walcott, P. O. Box A12, Georgetown.

'Uncle, can you get an officer to keep an eye on the Post Office Boxes? If Walcott or any one collects letters from Box A12, let him be arrested,' said James. His uncle agreed.

A detective was brought in, briefed, and posted to the General Post Office to see if anyone would try to retrieve any letters or other documents. Ruling out all possibilities of Anita being at the Hospital because of the diversions, the two cars and their cheerful occupants headed out of town towards the College Campus at Turkeyen.

Anita was anxiously waiting for them when they returned. She was sitting on the stairs of the multipurpose hall facing the parking lot. She ran to the car and lodged an immediate complaint. She wanted to know why Eddie was taken to that dreadful Georgetown Hospital. There were inadequate seating arrangements, no air conditioning and the toilet provisions were extremely poor. 'Why wasn't he taken to the Davis Memorial Hospital?' she inquired.

Her friends knew how particular she was about Eddie's welfare and recognizing the need for her to let out some steam, they allowed her to talk to ease some of the frustration. She further explained between sobs that she waited for about three hours at the hospital and the orderlies and armed guards refused to let her see her boyfriend.

Anita was of Amerindian and East Indian ancestry, so it was not difficult to see the reddening of her cheeks when she was upset, angry or frustrated. She often talked about the stories grandfather Harripaul told them about his father Baba Outar growing up in Madras before he was shipped out to Guyana to work on the sugar and rice fields as an indentured labourer. She could trace her Amerindian ancestry to Lethem.

When Anita had relaxed, Abiola coaxed her, 'But Anita, didn't James say that they may not allow you to see Eddie because of the circumstances?'

'I know, but why didn't you take him to a private hospital? After all, there wouldn't have been so many police officers and armed soldiers patrolling around. It was like he was a prisoner. I even told them that I was his girlfriend,' Anita explained.

'What did they say?' asked Shelly.

'What did they say, what did they say, absolutely nothing. It was as though I was speaking to stones and not human beings like myself. I felt so alone and embarrassed that I wanted to sneak out of the hospital at the earliest opportunity I got,' Anita informed them.

James tried to comfort her by explaining that it could have traumatized Eddie and caused psychological harm to him. Anita however was still peeved and went on to insist that they could have at least allowed her to give him a kiss on the cheek.

'Sure, if he was fit and healthy enough you could have,' Abiola said trying her best to console her.

'They didn't even accept the fruits that I took for him. All the mangoes, bananas and oranges I had to bring back to campus. Do you know what one of the police officers did when I asked to see Eddie?' she asked.

They all leaned forward in anticipation of the answer. 'Of all the cheeky idiotic things to do, that guy left me standing there, went to Eddie's room and returned with a picture which he handed to me,' she said.

They all laughed. 'Whose picture was it?' Henry asked.

'Mine,' she answered. 'The one I took with Eddie when we visited Kaieteur Falls in December, apparently Eddie had it in his wallet when they took him to the hospital.'

James and Henry had to suppress a smile since they were aware of the sentimental values girls attach to such things. Anita admitted that she was tempted to throw the bag of fruits at him but desisted only when she thought that she may have been arrested for assaulting a police officer and as she vividly put it, because he kept that long stupid gun across his chest as though waiting to use it on someone.

'About how many soldiers and police officers are there?' asked James.

'I really can't say how many but they are like flies standing there one moment, then alighting at another location in a jiffy. They surround the place like flies on a lump of brown sugar,' Anita said.

When they had finished consoling Anita as much as they could, they left her in the company of Abiola and Shelly and headed to Mr. Sam's office. Mr. Sam lived in the Principal's Residence on campus so he spent most of the time in his office and only went home to eat and sleep. He was one of the most loyal and dedicated educators and had received many National Awards for his contribution to the field of education.

The boys found Mr. Sam signing some documents. They brought him up to date on the happenings, thanked him for the use of his car and sought permission to use the radio sets for the holidays. He did not hesitate to grant them the use of all the radio sets and to assure them that they were free to use all the facilities of the college.

The boys got up to bid farewell when Mr. Sam asked them where they would be spending their vacation. James told him that his uncle had invited him and Henry to spend a few days at his home in Prashad Nagar. 'I guess he wants us to be close by until the mystery is solved.'

'I would have been glad to have you boys stay with me. You young cubs would have kept my old brains ticking,' Mr. Sam informed them.

'We'll visit you regularly; if we cannot visit we'll keep you informed by telephone, said Henry.'

Amidst praises and thanks for their efforts to solve the mystery, Mr. Sam begged them to be careful and always vigilant. The two boys shook hands with the principal, said good bye and left. They hurried to their rooms. They packed Eddie's belongings and their own into their respective suitcases, collected the girls and left the already deserted campus for Anita's home in South Ruimveldt Gardens.

Anita's family was expecting the boys, so immediately after introductions and unpacking some basic things, they were conducted to the dining room where they saw a table filled with all the delicacies they could think of. Labba curry, cook up rice, chowmein, shrimp fried rice, potato salad, ice cream and fruit cake. The food was inviting. The aroma tingled their nostrils. They all sat down bowed their heads and listened solemnly as Anita's mother opened the table with a prayer. She prayed for their safety, their success in college, their health and continued togetherness and friendship. When Anita's mother was finished they all said their amens and began small chatter. Henry and James brought the Applefarm's family up to date with the Mystery and Eddie's condition. The boys were careful to omit most of the details because Mrs. Applefarm was as emotional as her daughter Anita. She had lost her husband two years ago and this affected her. A friend had encouraged Daniel Applefarm to seek his fortune in the bush. He went to Imbaimadai to work as a pork knocker. He worked for a few months, contracted the dreaded malaria and returned to South Ruimveldt, where he died. Mrs. Applefarm took it very hard. This also affected Anita. They joined the Pentecostal Church on North Road and sought solace from the church community. It helped immensely and they were grateful. Every morning Matthew Allen, their neighbor, sent a special greeting and dedicated a religious hymn to Mrs. Applefarm and her church.

Mrs. Applefarm expressed horror at Eddie's near tragedy. One of her regrets was the fact that she had spent much time preparing Eddie's favorite banana pie topped with the best cherries she bought at Guyana Stores Supermarket. She was thankful to God, however, for preserving his life. She made a mental note to tell Prophet Cummings to pray for her family and especially Eddie.

Mrs. Applefarm told Anita to put on some soft religious music. She turned on the Greco set and inserted the cassette. The music was soothing and they chatted freely. After about an hour, the boys thanked Mrs. Applefarm for a hearty lunch. They praised her local five finger juice and coconut buns and Henry commented that it was the best labba curry he had ever eaten. Mrs. Applefarm beamed proudly; she prided herself on being an extremely good cook and at times would say that 'German' can never make a better cow heel soup than her.

Unfortunately, the boys could not spend the rest of the evening at the Applefarm's home so shortly after, they said their goodbyes and departed. 'You'll be seeing us soon,' Henry said as James turned the car and headed for Prashad Nagar where Supt. Clarke lived.

When they arrived, an old man opened the steel gate for them. He appeared to be an old retired police officer. It was almost standard practice for retired officers to work and do gardening and other chores for current officers. Both the Army and the Police Force had their culture and protected and looked out for their own.

'I'm the watch man,' the old man said, 'You are the Superintendent's nephew I presume, although he was expecting you earlier. No one is at home. His wife and kids are holidaying at a friend's ranch in the Rupununi. You are familiar with the home. Here are the keys. Make yourself at home and be comfortable,' the watch man told them.

They thanked him, took their suitcases and disappeared into the spacious house. Prashad Nagar was an affluent residential community and many influential politicians and other senior government officials lived there. They chose a breezy room with two beds and without bothering to unpack, they pulled off their tee shirts, jumped into bed and were soon fast asleep.

They woke in the early afternoon but strange enough their bodies felt as though they had absolutely no rest. James raised his hands over his head, extended his arms and yawned. James' yawning seemed contagious because Henry soon followed with his own. They relaxed on their beds and reminisced; each of them engrossed in his own thoughts. James wondered about Mr. Cheong, and the mystery. His mind flashed to Bernice and Keith and what had become of Alfie Walcott. Henry thought about Abiola, Shelly and Anita. He wondered how they were holding up to the developments and unfolding of the mystery. Both boys sighed almost simultaneously and sat upright.

Henry told James what he was musing over and James said that he was also doing some thinking of his own. 'Let's get something to munch on. I've eaten so much over the last few days but I still feel hungry, it's like I can eat a cow,' he said.

Henry laughed but agreed that he was also famished. They went to the kitchen where they prepared warm chocolate milk and helped themselves to coconut tarts and square cut. Over the hurriedly prepared snacks, James phoned Mrs. Applefarm's home and told the girls that they would pick them up to visit Eddie. The boys got dressed and half an hour later they were heading to the Applefarm's home. Although filled, the boys had to accept Mrs. Applefarm's offer of a small glass of sorrel drink. They reluctantly, but politely declined the offer of black cake.

Mrs. Applefarm shirked the offer to visit the hospital to see Eddie. She claimed that she had some church related activities to attend to. The boys expressed their regret that she couldn't make it. The girls giggled and seemed more amused than ever. She reminded them to tell Eddie that she loved him and to get well soon, because all of her food is being wasted. She smiled when she said that, knowing how much Edie loved her cuisine. The girls kissed Mrs. Applefarm and Henry and James hugged her. They then left for the hospital to visit Eddie.

The boys were bothered by the girls' reaction to Anita's mother not wanting to go to the hospital. When they were settled in the car Henry asked the reason. Abiola snickered and Shelly explained that Mrs. Applefarm was ghastly afraid that Anita would kiss Eddie in front of her and that was taboo. They all laughed loudly, but that was the reality. Some things were definitely out of the question and kissing in public was one of them. Even during marriage ceremonies, a crowd would gather around to get a good view after the priest, pastor or officiating officer announced that the groom may now kiss the bride. Cameras would flash, shouts would go up requesting an encore, do it again, I didn't see it, the oohs and aahs were deafening. In Guyana, that signaled the end of the marriage ceremony and relatives and mostly uninvited guests would head towards the eating area.

The boys now understood why the girls reacted that way since on many occasions the girls had to push them away when their parents were nearby. Abiola and James could remember vividly when her father would sit between Henry and Abiola when he visited her. Some parents inserted younger brothers and sisters to spy on what went on between siblings who were courting.

When the boys reached the hospital, they found that Supt. Clarke, Inspector Jordan, Brigadier Gillis and Lieutenant James were already there. Introductions were made all around. The girls were elated to have the opportunity to meet with the top brass in the Army and Police Force.

'We have decided to let you see your friend first,' said Brigadier Gillis.

'The doctors decided that your presence will do him much good. Then I think that he had been asking for one of the young ladies, Anita I think,' he feigned a smile.

Anita blushed and her cheek reddened. A doctor appeared and said that the patient was now ready to receive the first group of visitors. They did so eagerly. Eddie was sitting up on the edge of his bed wearing blue hospital pajamas. Anita rushed into his arms and kissed him passionately. She would have remained there hugging and squeezing him if the others did not remind her that Eddie would still be sore and hurting. She reluctantly released his neck but not before whispering in his ears that she loved him with all her heart.

Henry and James wondered how Mrs. Applefarm would have reacted to such emotion from her daughter. Later when alone, they concurred that she may have fainted or even have a heart attack.

Eddie managed a feeble smile and said that he was feeling much better but only the cut at the back of his head was bothering him. He turned slowly to show them the bandage just at the back of his head that we Guyanese call 'the greedy peep.'

'Who did this to you?' Anita asked.

Henry and James bent over to get all the details. 'You'll be surprised to know,' said Eddie, 'Alfie Walcott, a guy named Blackie, another called Antonio and my roommate Denny Bollers.'

They were astounded and filled with disbelief. 'Bollers,' they gasped almost in unison.

'Yeah, he's one of the gang and a very important one at that,' said Eddie. He then asked pointedly, 'Haven't you guys brought anything to eat?'

He told them that he had been surviving on a strict liquid diet but earlier in the afternoon he was given permission to take normal meals. Anita informed him that her mother had prepared and sent a special basket for him. Eddie was delighted as he took the treats from Anita. He opened it and started to eat. 'I am sorry that Supt. Clarke isn't here. There is so much to tell you guys,' he said between mouthfuls.

'They are all here waiting on the outside to speak with you. There is Supt. Clarke, the Commander of the Armed Forces, Inspector Jordan and a Lieutenant,' James said.

'Bring them in quickly, I feel tired and may fall asleep soon. The doctors said I lost quite a lot of blood and am very dehydrated,' he said.

At the mention of his condition Anita pulled a handkerchief from her hand bag and wiped away a tear. Abiola hugged her and rubbed her shoulder in sympathy. Shelly on the other hand walked over to Eddie and patted his shoulder and reassured him that everything would be all right. Eddie acknowledged their concern and gave a feeble smile.

Henry and James went outside to the waiting lounge and soon returned with the high powered delegation. The men entered in single file, their hats firmly tucked under their arms in true military style. They inquired about his health and wished him a speedy recovery. Eddie was visibly impatient and fidgeting, without waiting to be interrogated, he asked them to make themselves comfortable while he recounted the details of his ordeal.

He explained that it all started when he followed his roommate Denny Bollers, who had sneaked out of the dormitory and rendezvoused with Blackie and Ginger. Eddie shadowed them and saw them retrieve something dropped by a low flying airplane. He went on to say that Antonio and Alfie Walcott surprised him and Walcott struck him with the butt of a revolver at the back of his head.

The gathering listened attentively and without interruption. Eddie further told them, 'The next thing I knew, I was in a dark, foul smelling, dank room, bound hand and feet, and gagged with a piece of old rotten flour bag. Blackie and Antonio were assigned to guard me. Antonio radioed the boss and the boss told him to shoot me, but Antonio refused to let me have such a humane death. Said he saw a similar hanging as a mercenary in Africa. He and Blackie argued about it. Antonio's plan was to have me hang myself, that's the only reason why I am alive today. Antonio preferred the slow, agonizing death rather than the swift execution of a bullet through the heart as recommended by his boss.

'Antonio kicked me in the face and he and Blackie continued their argument. Blood streaked down my face and I thought that I was losing consciousness, Eddie said to the girls who at this point gasped at these revelations.

The girls could endure no more of the graphic details and were escorted out of the room by James. He left them in the lounge area and hurried back to Eddie's room. The superintendent wanted to know if Eddie had told them all he knew or if any important detail was omitted. Eddie said that Antonio claimed to have fought in Namibia, Mozambique and South Africa and he wondered if he had ever met the African freedom fighters and stalwarts like Bishop Desmond Tutu and Robert Mugabe. He claimed to have killed many men in the jungles of Nigeria during the Biafran war and even boasted that he had visited the legendary town of Soweto, the birth place of Nelson Mandella. Eddie also said that Antonio talked about war and uprising in Guyana. He recounted an airplane later came, landed then left and he was left perched on the wooden box and strapped to the chair.

'Is that all you heard and know?' asked the Lieutenant.

'Well, probably that's as much as I could remember,' said Eddie who was visibly tired and wanted to lie down.

They sensed that Eddie was in discomfort. The Brigadier commented that the situation was grave but a clearer picture had emerged about the situation. He nodded to the others, put a hand on Eddie's shoulders, thanked him for all the valuable information he had provided and left the room. The others also thanked Eddie and the Lieutenant said, 'Thank you boys; you have done a great service to your country. The enormity of it will only be known when this matter is concluded.'

'Indeed,' agreed Supt. Clarke, 'all we have to do is alert all our armed forces and be thoroughly prepared for any eventuality.'

Before leaving Eddie's room, James suggested that it may be more prudent to be ultra-secretive since the gang did not know that Eddie was still alive and unaware that so much information had been gleaned. They agreed and welcomed James' suggestion. 'If there is any uprising or disturbance I think that it would emanate from the Essequibo region. They have been very restive for a few months from what I heard. What if Henry and I fly out to the Rupununi area and do some investigating? The Dawana area seems to be the most likely hideout and headquarters of the gang.'

The group agreed wholeheartedly but when the girls learned about the proposed plan they rejected it outright. They were scared that their boyfriends would come to harm. However, the military men convinced them that it was beneficial to the entire nation. Reluctantly, they agreed and succumbed to reason. The group departed the hospital shortly after. The police officers and army personnel left as a group and James, Henry, Anita and Shelly decided to spend about an hour more with Eddie, who was fast asleep. They sat on chairs provided by the janitor, talked about a few activities to be undertaken when Eddie was discharged from the hospital and the wonderful time they had at the closing party.

There being no further reason to be at the hospital, each one of them kissed Eddie on the cheek in a good bye gesture, waved to the armed guards still stationed outside Eddie's room and left. An hour later, Henry and James dropped the girls off at the Applefarm's home. It was a very revealing and hectic day. The boys enjoyed most of it, but the girls were apprehensive. Abiola and Anita feared Antonio. Eddie's revelations had left an indelible mark on their minds.

The boys asked them to convey their regards to Mrs. Applefarm and to again thank her for her wonderful meal. James then headed to his uncle's home.

THE HIDDEN BOMB

Supt. Clarke phoned at around eight o'clock and told the boys to accommodate themselves because he may not be home for the night. The boys assured him of their competence and reliability, something that he was very sure about. He smiled when he thought of the young man whom he had taken in and adopted when his brother died and his mother followed shortly after. James however chose to live with his widowed grandmother on Durban Street. The boys prepared a light meal then settled down to a game of chess. They were studying the rudiments of chess from the Guyana chess champion and international master Alvin Rogers, who was also a college class mate. During the game Henry suggested that they give Mr. Sam a call to reassure him that they were okay and some progress had been made.

They dialed the principal's home number and he answered immediately as though he was expecting the call. They told him about Eddie's health and the girls worrying. However, they did not divulge any sensitive information about what they had learned from the senior police and military officers. Mr. Sam wanted to know how some people could be so barbaric but the boys could not proffer an answer.

'By the way, a young man was here to see Eddie,' Mr. Sam informed him.

'What did he want, did you ask him?' James asked.

'Sure I questioned him, he told me that he was a teacher at Kurupung and that he and Eddie were supposed to travel to Essequibo together,' Mr. Sam said.

'That's definitely not true. Eddie would never have made such plans without informing us. Moreover, we were planning to visit Bartica for the annual regatta,' James added.

'What did you tell him?' asked Henry.

'I have learned a few things from you my young sleuths, I let him know that Eddie had left since Thursday. He seemed pleased with my answer but then he asked for Eddie's two friends. I became suspicious and told him I did not know if Eddie had any friends on campus. It was then that he pulled out James' identification card from his pocket and showed it to me.'

'Wait a second, how did he get that? I gave it to a police officer when he stopped me at the Stabroek market in front of Demico House. My goodness, things were happening so quickly I forgot to take it back,' James said showing a rare sign of anxiety and genuine panic.

He asked for a brief description of the man, when Mr. Sam told him he said that he thought the individual was an impostor since he couldn't be a teacher and a police officer at the same time.

'I gave him all assurances that you will be here tomorrow at two o'clock so he could come in and return the identification card to you himself,' Mr. Sam informed him.

'Why did you ask him to return tomorrow?' Henry wanted to know.

'I realized that he was a crook and dishonest. His vocabulary was too limited and grammar too poor to be a teacher. That is what gave him away. Nothing like a good old fashion education,' laughed Mr. Sam.

'Good old Mr. Sam. I'll phone my uncle and let him prepare a trap to nab him if he does turn up to return my identification card,' James said.

They spoke a few more minutes with the principal, excused themselves and hung up the telephone. James called his uncle but he was unavailable. He then contacted Inspector James and told him of his conversation with Mr. Sam and asked him to get Supt.

Clarke and to set up a sting operation at the college campus. The inspector agreed to pass on the information immediately to the top brass. They thanked the inspector and hung up the telephone.

It was approaching midnight and the trials and travails of the day weighed heavily on the boys, so they got into bed, pulled their mosquito nets down, and settled down for a long and hopefully blissful night's sleep. Neither of them remembered to say the traditional Guyanese children's favorite night time prayer. 'This night when I lie down to sleep I give the Lord my soul to keep. If I should die before I wake, I give the Lord my soul to take, Amen.'

Both Henry and James wondered before their eyelids became too heavy to remain open what Mrs. Applefarm would have said if she knew that they went to bed without saying a prayer to the deity.

The night seemed hours shorter as the two boys awoke to find the room already bathed in the soft golden hue of sunrise. The sun in its brilliance hugged the Atlantic Ocean and slowly, majestically rose on its daily journey as it traversed the azure vista. They were so tired that neither of them heard the fowl cock crowing or the jumbie bird that had recently started making passes over grandfather Baboo Lall's house. Baboo Lall was ninety-four years old and nearing the point of death. Guyanese folklore has it that the black bird referred to as the jumbie bird is the forewarner of someone's demise.

The boys took a bath using a bucket and plastic bowl to dip and throw water on themselves because there was a black out and the water pump couldn't lift the water up to the overhead tank for them to use the shower. Henry then made bacon and scrambled eggs for breakfast, while James called the girls and outlined their activities for the day. Breakfast was tasty and good and Henry admitted that his culinary prowess was improving beyond the hard boiled eggs that he was accustomed making. 'One day I will try some rice pap with coconut milk or some corn meal with evaporated milk,' he promised.

James heard him and smiled because he knew that Henry would never face the stove for more than twenty minutes and rice pap would take about an hour or more unless you got the good soft white rice from the La Penitence or Bourda Market. There was a wider choice of rice unless you wanted to have to pick paddy and rock from that sold by the local market vendors and shop owners like slick Khan, Benjie Yhap or Buddy Boy Singh. Slick Khan had the reputation for mixing white flour with milk powder and selling it as pure powered milk. Rumour also had it that he was mixing his curry powder with sifted saw dust. Many people only bought madras and indi curry because they were only sold in sealed packages.

After speaking with the girls, the boys headed to the college to see if any progress had been made with apprehending the impostor who swiped James' identification card. When they arrived on campus they discovered that he had already been apprehended by four plain clothes detectives who had tricked him into thinking that they were the principal's sons who were visiting him for his birthday.

He was whisked away to the Brickdam Police station, interrogated for an hour and put behind bars. He begged for his one constitutional phone call to let his supposed wife know that he had been arrested. The constable gave him a phone and he complained that the phone wasn't working. The constable took the telephone, looked at him and said in a clear military tone, 'Man, this is Guyana, not America where everything works.'

The impostor gripped the iron bars and contemplated his situation. The realization then hit him like a ton of bricks that he would soon be at the maximum security prison complex in Camp and Durban streets behind the foreboding 14 foot steel sheet barricade topped by razor and barbed wire for a very long time. He bowed his head and began crying like a baby. The interrogators later claimed that the only information he divulged was his nickname, Polo. They thought that he was a low level operative but nothing was to be taken for granted until the case was solved.

Supt. Clarke, as he had indicated, did not return home that night, so James called him. He was fully apprised of all the details and said that they had already gotten two suspects they were aggressively interrogating but they were not divulging any information. He said that they were either well trained or were not very significant to the operation. He informed James that they may be, what is called in military terminology, 'collateral,' someone who could be gotten rid of or killed if he is no longer beneficial to the operation.

James heard the telephone ring, so he knew that his uncle was busy. He put him on hold and answered the second line. He spoke briefly, hung up and informed James that the call was from Brigadier Gillis at army headquarters informing him that the detachment of men had resumed excavation work at the site at Dawana. He explained that the only development was that the resident native Amerindian population had become very hostile. His uncle then hung up and asked him to call him back later with any additional information or to receive reports of any new developments in the case. After briefing Henry on what his uncle told him James cupped his chin and tried to figure out why the normally docile, friendly natives, would suddenly resort to open hostility. Henry looked at him and told him to stop propping sorrow. The remark sounded just like his grandmother Cousin Hepsie.

James was pensive and thought about what could have angered the Amerindians. Henry was also in deep concentration. As was his habit he placed his right hand on his forehead and began massaging his eyebrows. 'Whatever can be happening in the Essequibo?' he asked James.

James admitted that he was at a total loss as to the reason. The tribal leaders have always been helpful. He started to name the most significant tribes and their locations to ascertain if he could identify a pattern. There was the Patamonas of South Rupununi, where old Kaie their chief, after whom the world famous Kaieteur Falls was named, the Akawaios of upper Mazaruni, Pomeroon and Cuyuni Rivers, the Wai-Wai and Macushi of south and North Rupununi, the

Arawaks who gave us the cassava based piwari and cassava bread, the Arecunas of Kamarang, the Wapishana, the Warraus and Caribs who were expert trackers and canoe makers.

Henry listened in awe as James rattled off the names of the tribes and their locations; there was no need to ask. James was always traveling throughout the Essequibo region and had even made treks along the Canje Creek as far as Baracara and walked across to Kimbia and Kwakwani. Rumour had it that he was trying to get to Essequibo by accessing the Mahdia Trail.

Henry offered an opinion after James' expository, 'The natives may have realized that their livelihoods and welfare were being threatened by the work of Mr. Cheong,' Henry said. 'We should not forget that for many years the only contact the natives had with civilization was through the many white Catholic missionaries. They trusted them implicitly and even the national government had to use them as intermediaries in sensitive negotiations such as land disputes.' James concurred and added that they were also a superstitious people who may for some unknown reason were being instigated into such action.

Meanwhile, back at the police headquarters, another call came in for the superintendent. The caller at the other end of the line identified himself as detective Corporal Alexander. The police officer reported that a man had gone to PO Box A12 and had collected two letters, when challenged he tried to escape but was apprehended after a brief pursuit. Detective Corporal Alexander further said that the man like the two other captured gang members when captured only gave his name, Dwarka. The letters were asked to be taken to headquarters immediately and the boys were asked to report to Eve Leary. They arrived not long after, and soon James, his uncle and Henry were peering over the letters. The first was stamped at the Rose Hall Post Office, Corentyne, Berbice. It was a reminder to pay a debt of thirty dollars to shopkeeper Manuel Veira. The second letter was posted in the United States from Maryland state.

James picked up the letter and read it to the others. It said,

15-23 Washington Avenue
Lincoln Square, MD 3031211

Dear Daddy,

As you know, I am graduating from Howard University next year. Everything is fine, I really appreciate the package and money you sent for me. I'll be home for Christmas, but remember Daddy I want a dreamy orange parakeet for my birthday. Give my regards to all at home.

Your loving daughter,
Gracie.

'Don't you think it is too short and bland for a daughter to a father?' asked Henry.

'It can be that the relation between them is not too good,' suggested Supt. Clarke.

'But, what does she want with an orange parakeet, and how would she get it to the states with all these new protections and restrictions on wild life exportations?' asked Henry.

James was absolutely convinced that the letter must be a coded message. Henry and the superintendent agreed and they decided to spend some time deciphering the suspected coded letter. They juggled the words and substituted numbers for letters but didn't arrive at anything tangible. James' uncle sought the comfort of one of his favourite cigars which he extracted from a silver case adorned with the coat of arms. The boys on the other hand sipped on ice cool pineapple juice and ate sweet biscuits that a receptionist brought in.

Supt. Clarke telephoned Brigadier Gillis and told him about the latest developments. 'I have been briefing Prime Minister Joseph

Ross and he has expressed great anxiety. I have also advised him to cancel all public appearances for fear of attacks on his life. He was particularly disappointed about not being able to attend the three o'clock inauguration of the National Amerindian Development Council at the Umana Yana or the Police Male Voice Choir recital at the National Cultural Centre. He recognized the enormity of the situation to national security and agreed to follow all the instructions of the security experts.'

After speaking to the Brigadier, Supt. Clarke returned to the boys who looked pensive still pouring over the coded letter. He asked if they had made any progress. He was given a negative waving of the head. James immediately regretted his gesture toward his uncle. He remembered that it was impolite to shake your head or hands at your elders when answering questions or communicating with them.

James looked up from the letter and said that he may have found a possible clue. 'Let us examine this particular sentence, DADDY I WANT A DREAMY ORANGE PARAKEET and the number 3031211 Washington.'

'Yes, continue,' Henry encouraged.

'Can't you recognize the pattern, the sentence has letters and numbers digits take the first three letters from DADDY you get DAD, no letter from the second, three letters from the third WANT, you get WAN,' said James.

Henry took a typewriting sheet and with help from his friend reconstructed the words. It read DADWANA. The same was done with DREAMY ORANGE PARAKEET, that spelt DR .... O .... P. There it was they all saw the coded message revealed before their eyes. 'DAWANA DROP.'

James' uncle couldn't help but marvel at his nephew's intuitiveness. He wondered if he shouldn't encourage him to give up teaching and join the Police Officer Cadet School. *With James' skills and my connections it would not be difficult to study at Scotland Yard*, thought the Superintendent. However, he couldn't force James into being what he wanted. He remembered his neighbor, Mr. Yassim, and how his son wanted to be an accountant, although Mr.

Yassim always wanted a doctor in his family. He discouraged his son Mohammed and shipped him off to England to study medicine. Mohammed rebelled and only attended classes for a week, he dropped out and gave Mr. Yassim many grandchildren after he hooked up with Indra Yacoob, a Pakistani girl from Karachi, who had run away from an arranged marriage.

'There would be some sort of drop at Dawana' reasoned the superintendent, 'the thing is when and where.'

'This is what I can't figure out. Nothing in the message gives any hint or clue, so it seems as though we may have to get to Dawana earlier than anticipated,' said James.

Both Henry and his uncle agreed. Supt. Clarke again telephoned his counterpart at the army headquarters. When he got on to the Commander, he informed him that the message had been decoded and there would be some sort of drop at Dawana. The commander acknowledged the possibility and promised to make a helicopter and crew available the following day to fly James, Henry and Keith to Dawana for further investigations. The boys left the police headquarters shortly after.

On their way home they stopped at the National Food Services Cooperative and helped themselves to an appetizing meal. When they were finished dining, they ordered a portion of fried shark and yellow tailed trout to take for the girls. They got to the car, entered and headed for the Applefarm's home.

'James, I thought I saw you close the car when we went to get our food,' Henry said.

'Yes, I believe that I did, but it was opened. I don't make that mistake, even if I am in a hurry,' James said with an air of concern.

'Then someone must have tampered with the car while we were eating.'

James brought the car to a hurried stop and said that they had better check it out to be on the safe side. They searched the back seat and under the front seats. Henry opened the dash board compartment and discovered to their horror, a neatly wrapped package. They both heard a distinct ticking sound emanating from the package and instantly knew that it was a timed bomb. There was an ominous silence and it appeared that time stood still. Henry picked up the package carefully, his hands shaking and sweaty. There was a moment of hesitation as the boys stared death in the face. Henry ignored the oncoming traffic, ran blindly across the road and hurled the package into the West Ruimveldt Recreation Field as he shouted to James to lay on his stomach and cover his ears.

Seconds later the ground shook violently under a massive explosion. Passersby ran to their assistance as dirt, debris and the southern fence were uprooted.

'Are you okay?' a senior citizen asked, as he helped Henry to his feet.

'Yes, I am all right,' he said, 'although I nearly lost my life.'

'Believe me son, I nearly lost my heart,' the man retorted.

After assuring the crowd that they were in fine shape, they accepted the offer of a middle aged woman who lived nearby to use her telephone. Henry and James accompanied her to a white wooden bungalow and she took off the padlock from the door and invited them in. Inspector Jordan received the call and after hearing of the boy's narrow escape, promised to contact the Local Authority Office to effect repairs as early as possible. They thanked the woman and left. To their amazement, they saw a group of residents armed with shovels, hammers and fencing materials preparing to replace the fence. They hurried across the field and after spending an hour with the residents, they returned to the car. James gasped in horror at a warning posted on the windshield and held in place by the windshield wiper. It read, 'LUCKY BITCHES, WE'LL GET YOU!'

'I don't think we should tell the girls about the bomb scare and this warning, they will worry to death,' said Henry. They reached home still shaken.

The old watch man greeted them warmly, 'Hi fellas, the three girls were here. About an hour ago said they were going to the hospital, and they left these lunch packets for you.'

They thanked him, collected the packets and hurried to their room. They listened to the seven o'clock newscast and were surprised to hear the newscaster end by announcing that two teenagers narrowly escaped death in a bomb attack, however, no names were mentioned.

'Wonder if the girls are listening?' asked James.

'We'll soon know,' laughed Henry, just then the phone rang. 'There goes.'

Henry picked up the phone. 'Are you guys all right?' Anita's voice sounded wavering.

'All in one piece,' he answered. 'By the way, why do you ask?'

'Don't pretend. We were listening to the news and we heard of a bomb attack. We knew immediately you were the boys involved,' she said.

Unwillingly, they had to give the determined girls the details of the attack and the other developments.

'Can't tell you everything over the phone, someone may be listening to our conversation.'

James also reassured the girls that there was no need for undue anxiety. 'We enjoyed the cassava biscuits and plantain chips,' he said.

'So did the sick,' answered Abiola. 'Even rebuked us for not taking more.'

'We'll turn in early. Have a good night's rest,' James said, as he put the receiver onto its hook.

'I didn't even remember that tomorrow we're flying to Dawana,' said Henry. 'Did you tell the girls of our trip to Dawana?'

'Oh yes, we had better start packing.'

By eight-thirty, they were finished and relaxing. 'We should get accustomed to a few country and western tunes.'

'Fine, that's what they listen to in the interior. Charlie Pride, Dolly Parton, Willie Nelson and others,' said James, as he selected a few long playing albums from his uncle's collection.

'What about some wine?'

'Here's a bottle marked piwari,' said James, taking a green banko bottle out of the refrigerator. 'This is the ideal thing.'

They drank the piwari and sang until they felt sleepy. 'Not a bad night,' said Henry, as he turned the lights off and dived head first into bed. They were awakened by the ringing of the telephone. Henry touched James sleepily.

'You answer it,' he yawned. James glanced at the bed side clock. It showed half past three.

He hurried into the sitting room and lifted the receiver. 'This is Supt. Clarke there has been an important development. I will be away for a week. Report to army headquarters tomorrow and prepare to travel to Dawana, that's all.'

He hung up. James was baffled. He told Henry what his uncle had said. 'We'll figure that out tomorrow,' Henry answered as he again yawned and pulled his blanket over his head. They woke early, phoned the girls and drove to army headquarters.

HENRY DISAPPEARS

At the army headquarters, every detail had been set. Shortly after, the two boarded the helicopter along with Captain Persaud and Keith.

'Goodbye, Georgetown,' Henry laughed, as they streamed over St. George's Cathedral, 'Wow! The City is more picturesque from the air,' he shouted, as he snapped a few pictures. He was amazed at the architecture of St. George's Cathedral which was designed by Arthur Bloomfield and completed in 1892. Standing at an impressive 43.5 meters, he was proud Guyana claimed the tallest wooden structure in the world.

Keith and James chatted about recent developments. Keith also hinted that Lieutenant James was away on a secret mission to the United States. James wondered if this had any connection with his uncle's hurried departure. They soon had the rural settlements under them.

'Wow, look at the cane and rice fields,' Henry again sighed. There were hundreds of thousands of acres and the plowing season had just begun, so dozens of Ferguson and Ford tractors were out chugging through and turning the soil.

They headed for Bartica, the mecca of Guyana's regatta. The lakes and the rivers increased, as they headed further inland. Houses were scarce, but there were the ever increasing dense forests and hills. From Bartica, they headed for Mahdia then to Kaieteur Falls. The splendor of the waterfall with its perpendicular, cascading 230 meters drop, against the blue horizon and green luxuriant forestry was fascinating.

'It's a pity the coastal folks don't come this way,' said James, as Captain Persaud landed at Karasabi to refuel.

'Why?' asked Keith, who had been sleeping for the greater part of the journey.

'Because they'll give up the drab coastland for the exciting hinterland,' he said.

'Yeah, whenever I want to settle down, I'll buy a piece of land this way,' Keith said.

'Not a bad idea,' admitted Henry, to the native Amerindian. 'Whenever I decide to settle down it would be a sign for the world to prepare for judgment.'

'Henry, don't forget that Abi is my cousin,' James teased, 'She's expecting you to do so soon,' he added, patting Henry on the shoulder.

Refueling took fifteen minutes and they were soon back in the air and heading for Lethem. Half an hour later they were navigating the Kanuka Mountains.

'Dawana is situated around this mountain range,' Captain Persaud said.

'No wonder, these mountains provide ideal hideouts,' said Henry.

Captain Persaud circled the area, then landed. They were immediately surrounded by anxious natives and the soldiers who were flown out to supplement Mr. Cheong's depleted work force.

A middle-aged, short, but broad shouldered Chinese approached them.

'Glad you came, Ernest,' he said.

'You look healthier than ever Mr. Cheong,' replied Captain Persaud, 'and this is my precious cargo James Clarke, Henry Major and Sergeant Keith Whyte.'

After the introductions, Mr. Cheong took them on a tour of the camp. There were tents strewn over an area of about a hundred meters, fragments of rock and stone implements adorned the sandy ground. Surrounding the camp was a wide expanse of tropical forests, and over to the north and south were peaks of mountains.

'This place gives me the creeps,' said Henry timidly. 'Snakes, tigers and cougars may be hiding in those forests and looking at us this very moment.'

The others were amused and laughed. Mr. Cheong then conducted the three to their tents on the eastern edge of the camp, not far from where the helicopter was parked. 'Make yourselves comfortable. In this part of the country, there isn't even the need to be clothed,' he said jovially. 'It's hot and there isn't anyone to tell you that it's indecent.'

Mr. Cheong then gave an account of the latest developments. He told of attacks made on the workers by the native Amerindians and of a mysterious mountain hideout where he believed a European was holding a few natives under subjugation. He claimed he was running a Cooperative Farm, but no farming could be done on this arid mountain soil.

'Sounds interesting,' James said. 'Since we have the helicopter at our disposal, what if we view the mountain by air?'

'I have a guide who knows that area well,' said the archeologist. 'I can get him to point out a few places.'

They agreed. 'Do you have any other guides?' Henry asked.

'Yes, there is another, but I don't trust him,' he said, 'I caught him snooping in the stockroom.'

'You must point him out to us, since he may be valuable,' Keith voiced.

The reliable guide was brought and invited on the helicopter trip. When everything was in place, Captain Persaud took off rising vertically in the wonder craft and heading towards the mountain. They circled the mountain twice in the fading light, but saw nothing, not even a suitable landing site, so they returned to camp.

They had a taste of bush hog curry and brown rice prepared by an army cook who proved to be a master of the art of cooking. After dinner, the trio retired to bed, anticipating a rough day ahead. The night was extremely cold, so they had to substitute their inadequate blankets for the more comfortable sleeping bags. They tucked their feet into the bags and carefully ascended on to the hammocks suspended above the ground by four forked sticks and six straight poles. Their makeshift beds proved more comfortable than they had first imagined and soon they were sleeping. They were too tired to think of the girls or even to say their prayers.

Mr. Cheong woke them up early the next morning. 'Rise friends! This is not Georgetown. You know, if you sleep too much, tigers may carry you off and you don't realize it until they're patting your face with their paws,' he joked.

The boys turned pale at the thought of being stroked playfully by a big striped cat. 'Guyana is part of the great Amazonian region and as such its jungles and rain forests are replete with wild life. The richness and fertility of its land, coupled with expansive water ways, rivers, waterfalls, tributaries, lakes, creeks and islands will surely one day support an industry of Eco-Tourism,' said Mr. Cheong cheerfully.

The boys crawled out of their sleeping bags and Henry asked for some water to bathe. 'Yeah, there's a lake just off the track you may use that, but don't expect it to be hot and cold like Lake Itiribisi,' Mr. Cheong said. His mood and demeanour had improved since the contingent had arrived. He was becoming his usual happy, jovial self again. 'The water we keep on site is only for drinking and emergency.'

Excited and intrigued by the thought of swimming in a lake, the boys grabbed their towels and bath soap and headed towards the lake at a slow jog. The path wound under overhanging tree branches and seemed paved by dry fallen leaves. The occasional small animal scampered across the track and from the canopy of the trees marmosette monkeys swung from branch to branch using their tails as slings. The boys jogged for about a meter, walked another mile before they saw the massive lake appear before them. It glistened in the slanting rays of the morning sun. Guyana was certainly the Land of many Waters.

'If this is just along the track, I sure wouldn't like to see what is far along the track,' laughed Henry as he kicked off his boots and prepared to dive into the lake.

They swam for half an hour then returned to camp where they immediately sought Mr. Cheong. 'I thought that you said the lake was just along the track,' Henry commented.

Mr. Cheong grinned widely, 'You'll get used to it, and fall into the habit of taking a bath once a week and even that may prove too regular for you. Some pork knockers take a bath when they are coming in to the bush and take one when they are going out months after.'

'How was your initiation to the lake? Did you enjoy the morning stroll?' asked Keith.

'So you knew about it. It's a long time since I walked so far!' said James

'Yes, of course I knew, I lived and worked in the interior. They measure and talk about distances differently in these parts that's what they call a bush man's mile.'

They had a simple bushman's breakfast of break o' day biscuits, salt butter, boiled eggs and cassava bread, which they dipped in some left over pepperpot. They then began making preparations to visit the work site. Mr. Cheong saw one of the Carib guides and informed the boys that he had been acting strangely and was found snooping and eavesdropping on numerous occasions.

'He looks suspicious in his movements and the shifting eyes always give a dishonest person away,' Henry said.

He remembered what his grandmother always said that the only people who don't make eye contact are crooks, thieves, liars, cheaters and the loose women around Tiger Bay and Main Street.

It was time for Captain Persaud to depart for Georgetown, so they went to see him at the helicopter. He did his routine safety checks, climbed aboard, gave them the thumbs up and salutary wave and gently maneuvered the helicopter away from the camp. He made an exquisite 'banked turn' waved, and headed off in the distance.

Just as the helicopter departed, the guide whose name was given as Buckie edged closer and closer into the forest, until he was engulfed by the greenery. James was with Mr. Cheong. Henry, however, saw Buckie's departure and followed. Buckie knew the forest well and did not hesitate a moment as he penetrated deeper and deeper into the undergrowth.

Where's he heading? Henry wondered, as he slipped behind some greenheart and mora trees to avoid detection.

After fifteen minutes, they entered a clearing and the peaks of the Kanuku Mountains loomed directly in their path. Buckie suddenly looked over his shoulder. Henry flung himself behind a tree. He peeked and to his horror, a coiled snake was looking him in the eyes. The coloured mass was camouflaged against the nut brown, parched leaves and the yellowish undergrowth. He was petrified. The jaws of the snake expanded. The eyes were electrifying. Henry appeared hypnotized. The fangs of the six foot reptile were bare and glittering, and the forked tongue waved menacingly.

Henry said softly, 'Lord, is this the way I must die?' as he closed his eyes. It occurred to him then that snakes were blind and that it was using its fangs to determine his location. He lay absolutely still and began mumbling the Lord's Prayer.

Suddenly there was a 'twang.' The reptile uncoiled as it careered through the air embracing death, a well-timed arrow through its head. Henry forgot Buckie momentarily, as he looked around for his benefactor. He soon appeared, an Amerindian youth about thirteen years old. Henry thanked him and hurried after Buckie. The boy sped after him.

'No! Don't go into the mountain,' he warned. 'Wicked men live there, Adai, adai,' the boy shouted in a strange dialect as they reached the base of the mountain.

'Do you know Mr. Cheong?' Henry asked.

'Yes,' he said, 'agi tita, agi tita. He's a good boss, he's a good boss.'

'I go after bad man if no return, tell him that I gone after man in mountain,' Henry replied in broken English.

The boy nodded. Henry had not gone far up the mountain's face when he heard a rumbling sound. He looked up and yelled in alarm as rocks and boulders began tumbling slowly towards him. He sought shelter behind a ledge but this was ripped apart by the avalanche of falling rocks. The boy watched horrified as loose earth and rock tumbled towards Henry. He was struck by a huge rock and between consciousness, he thought he saw men armed with guns descending towards him, but this was no illusion.

The boy saw the avalanche and the armed men descending towards Henry. He was well concealed and from his hiding place he saw two men seize Henry as three others made a crude stretcher, laid him on it and began their track back up the mountain. He waited a few minutes crouching and when he thought it was safe he scurried away from the dreaded area, towards the safety of Mr. Cheong's camp.

James was looking at a few of the Rock Paintings that Mr. Cheong had discovered. 'They look interesting,' he said.

'Not only interesting, but valuable,' Mr. Cheong informed him proudly. 'I think somewhere around here lies the burial ground of hundreds of tons of gold and diamonds,' the old archeologist continued.

'Wow!' said James in utter amazement.

'Yes, fantastic, but true!' he said. 'From researching, I would say that the most advanced community of Amerindians lived around here. Their crafts suggest this. Some date right back to the first and second century.'

'Henry should hear this,' said James, 'I wonder where he is?'

Mr. Cheong continued, 'For some reason the Indians began to die off and not wanting to leave their wealth for others to find, they collected the gold, diamonds and other precious articles and buried them in small quantities. I have found some of these, but from data collected and processed, I think there is a much larger collection somewhere, something like the riches of King Eldorado.'

'How did you know where to dig?' asked James.

'By reading the signs on the rocks,' he explained. 'The rock paintings express the way of life and the beliefs of the people. There are lizards, snakes, forms of their gods and human forms. These complicated stone engravings when put together express the feelings, religious beliefs and life of the people and their entire customs. Look at these,' he said handing a slip of paper to James.

'Is this a message?' James asked.

'Yes, it is and it says no one must go beyond this point,' Mr. Cheong explained.

'But in which direction?' asked James.

'The position of the sun tells that, if it's to the right, that means East, when it's to the left that's the west. When the sun is at the center of the picture it means north and when an animal looks away from the sun it means south.'

'Do you have or know of any other paintings on the other side of the Mountain range?' James asked.

'Yes, there are. These signs are found around rivers, mountains, waterfalls and rapids possibly in all the areas where the Indians lived,' he said, 'but why ask?'

'Is it possible for the paintings to have a hidden message suggesting the location of the great find you spoke about.'

'I never thought of that,' Mr. Cheong admitted.

'We are in the North Rupununi, over the Kanuku is the South Rupununi, then there are rock paintings on both sides,' he said. 'Isn't it possible for both sets of Rock Paintings to have a common link somewhere; possibly in the mountain?'

Mr. Cheong straightened up. 'I think you can be right. If that is so, we may need these.'

He handed James a few crude sketches. He pocketed all the available sketches and left. He scouted around the camp and asked the workers if they had seen Henry, but no one did. He started to become worried. It was not usual for Henry to wonder off without informing him, especially in thickly forested areas.

The news was quickly spread around the camp that Henry was missing. It was also discovered that the guide Buckie had disappeared. Three search parties were organized to comb the area, but they returned three hours later without success.

'Sure looks dim for Henry.' said Keith.

'What if we leave early tomorrow morning and head for the mountains?' suggested James. 'That spooky place can hold many secrets.'

Just then a middle aged Amerindian wearing feathers and beads appeared with a much younger companion.

'Can I see Mr. Cheong?' he asked in perfect English.

When Mr. Cheong appeared the man approached him and began speaking in his native dialect. The group was astonished hearing the guttural sounds and shrill tones that the man uttered. He frequently pointed to the youth and to the mountains.

'This man says that his son saw a man from this camp nearly killed by an avalanche as he followed an Amerindian into the mountains,' Mr. Cheong translated.

'By Jove, it's Henry!' James exclaimed.

The boy was questioned and in broken English and frequent Macusi phrases, he told of Henry's snake incident to the bewildered group and that some men came down the mountain and ferried him away in a makeshift stretcher. The boy told the gathering that the injured young man may be dead.

THE MYSTERY UNFOLDS

'No. It can't be! He's not dead, he's not dead!' said James visibly shaken up. 'It's a trick, he's been captured!' he shouted.

A search party was again organized and equipped with James' transmitting set, torchlights and guns. They again set out this time under the guidance of the three Carib Indians who were expert jungle trackers. Rain began falling rendering the narrow leafy trail a mass of mud and slush. In the forest night and darkness falls earlier than usual. This evening was no exception; nevertheless, they slowly clawed and groped their way through the insect and animal infested forestry.

'This is where I shoot the snake that nearly killed your friend,' said the young guide.

He went down on his knees and pointed as he shone the torchlight on the immobile form. He held up his hand and backed off, slowly motioning the search party all the time to make a detour around the fallen reptile. Everyone was confused but followed instructions. When they had safely negotiated the obstacle the chief guide explained that some snakes move in pairs and when one is killed the other moves it, then takes the exact position and attacks the next person who takes the same path. He also informed the boys that some reptiles stalk humans for days or weeks when their mate is killed just to exact revenge. Everyone except the Amerindians cringed at the thought of being trailed by such large creeping creatures.

'What do you do since you have to live among them?' asked James.

'We see them as part of our environment and treat them accordingly. We don't kill them, we leave them alone. You can only survive in the forest if you understand the laws of the jungle,' the senior guide said.

The slushy muddy track opened into a rough rocky path which they followed until it crisscrossed into a ravine. The guide said that this was Henry's general direction. 'This is Snake Mountain,' said the elder Amerindian guide. 'Dangerous during the day, and much more at night.'

They came to the mountain and immediately began clawing their way up its face their bodies silhouetted against the dark steep incline. The ground under their feet soon became loose and Keith suggested that there seemed to have been a land slide recently. The rain had stopped and on examining the ground they realized that the gravel had shifted. They were cold and dripping wet but they couldn't stop their trek. The moon had not emerged and the darkness formed a huge blanket extending as it seemed to eternity. They put out the beams of their flash lights and were moving in utter darkness and silence for fear of detection.

'This is where I saw your friend dead,' said the younger guide. 'I the know location by that ledge, there was a wall there, but it broke off by the falling rocks,' he explained very good English.

They surveyed the area using a single torchlight but to no avail. Henry was not to be found. Suddenly, James saw a glitter in the darkness. He was sure he was on to something. He surged forward but strong arms held him back. 'Don't move, that's a tiger looking for food,' said the old Amerindian who noted, when traveling, his name was Dukan and the younger guide his son was named Carlos.

James panted heavily, 'How do you know?' he asked turning to his rescuer, but Dukan and his son had disappeared in the darkness.

'Don't move any of you,' ordered Mr. Cheong. 'They have gone after the big cat,' he said.

Moments later, two human shapes were seen above the ledge on which the tiger crouched noiselessly waiting patiently for a possible kill. Arrows were fitted incredibly fast to the two bows the Amerindian carried. A split second later the tiger roared aloud then louder, its last, as it tumbled to the depths beneath, shot by expert archers.

'We'll collect the skin tomorrow,' said the proud Carlos, as he and his father returned to the search party.

'That's if it is still there. It will make a good feast for the other forest predators,' said Dukan.

It was later being evident to the search party that chances of locating Henry were slim to nonexistent in the increasing darkness so they agreed to abandon their search. It was then that Keith pointed to a faint light in the distance. 'Look there! That light, isn't it an airplane?'

They all stopped and listened peering into the moonless sky. It was definitely an airplane. As it came closer, lights started flashing from below. They were certainly signals emanating from the valley below. From their vantage point on the shoulder of the mountain, they could see the outline of what appeared to be a runway faintly lit by individuals carrying flash lights.

The lights ran parallel for about three hundred meters. 'Let's get closer,' Mr. Cheong suggested.

With the guidance of the Amerindians, they edged closer until they were directly above the make shift landing strip.

'Mr. Cheong,' said James, 'I would like to investigate this further. Use the radio set in my bag, tell army headquarters that Henry is missing and that I'm investigating a landing in the mountain. Keith and Dukan, can you come with me?'

The two men nodded agreeing to follow James. Dukan left his son as the guide for the rest of the search party, who would descend to camp with Mr. Cheong. As they said farewell to the search party, the men and James disappeared into the darkness with the elder Amerindian leading the way. James and his companions edged their way down the slopes and ledges until they were on the west of the illuminated strip. There were voices and movement among the rocks. This place was ideal for a hideout. It was completely obscured, hidden between two mountains and could only be observed from above. The plane could not have been seen from Mr. Cheong's camp and the sound of the powerful engines was lost in the vastness of the mountains and forestry. James remembered the coded letter sent to Walcott. His thoughts raced to Henry, would he be kept prisoner in the mountain hideout or flown out when the plane departed? He aimed to find out at all cost.

The plane cut throttle, circled twice, then landed. They crept closer and closer. Figures emerged from the darkness and approached the plane. He recognized a white face. 'That must be a European!' The door in the fuselage opened and a rope ladder was attached and thrown out. Men started climbing down; he counted them, five in all. They shook hands with the European then turned around. The glow of the lights shone in their faces. James stared openmouthed, flanking the European were faces he recognized, traitors to Guyana's nationhood.

'Alfie Walcott and Denny Bollers,' he whispered to Keith.

'The others must be the ones who captured Eddie,' said Keith, 'Blackie, Antonio and Ginger.'

From their vantage point, they saw the five disappear into the confines of the dark and hospitable valley.

'What must we do now?' asked Dukan.

'I have a slight suspicion that they would be loading that plane with stuff,' said James.

His fears were soon justified. Amerindians bearing baskets and packages began trekking towards the plane. The pilot, who was still in the craft, counted the parcels and packages as they were brought out.

'Dukan, suppose you join those Amerindians? They wouldn't recognize you in the dark,' said James. 'Find out anything you can about our friend and when the plane would be leaving,' he instructed.

'Bring the last parcel here,' called Keith after the cooperative and amicable Amerindian, who was already disappearing in the darkness. Keith and James sat on two boulders in the darkness and waited for Dukan's return.

✱ ✱ ✱

Meanwhile, Mr. Cheong had reached camp. He searched through the boy's tent until he found the radio set. He followed James' instructions and was soon on the army headquarters

Frequency. He flashed the message to the Radio Room. He was told to instruct the boys and that help would be flown out soon. Mr. Cheong replaced the radio and was returning to his quarters when he saw a blazing arrow streaking towards the stockroom. Others saw it too and raced to the stockroom, extinguishing the fire before it had even enveloped the fibre wrapped arrow. A message was found strapped to the shaft. It read ...

WE HAVE YOUR FRIEND
WE'LL GET YOU!
TELL US WHERE TO FIND
THE WEALTH OF THE MOUNTAIN
OR NEVER SEE HIM AGAIN!

Mr. Cheong read the scribbled message then tucked it into his jeans. No one from the camp slept peacefully that night, not only from fear of being attacked again, but also in expectation for the return of the remnants of the search party and Henry, the missing sleuth.

Back in the valley, Dukan left the wrapped package with James and Keith and reported that they had to unload something from the plane. He again disappeared in the darkness. The group was now working in complete darkness. The Amerindians moved with ant like precision. After what seemed ages, Dukan again returned this time with a longer package.

'This looks like a gun,' he said as he put the package into Keith's hand.

'Last trip,' he said. 'They are speaking of a special cargo,' he whispered, as he skipped off again.

Keith looked at James hardly making out his slim features in the darkness. 'Wonder if the special cargo is Henry,' he said.

'I was thinking of the same thing, in that case we'll snatch him before the plane leaves,' James said thoughtfully.

Dukan returned in high spirits. 'It's your friend,' he whispered. 'Four of us carried him to the plane and threw him in the cargo hold. He's all tied up; I even called his name when the others had departed.'

'Who is left with him?' asked Keith.

'Only the pilot, he said he was thirsty and to get him some water,' Dukan said.

'What if we surround and jump him?' Keith said.

'That may not be the best thing to do. He may call for back up and have the entire gang on us in no time,' James said thoughtfully.

'I have an idea,' Dukan said. 'What if I get the water and put some drugs inside to make him sleep.'

The idea appealed to all so Keith asked where they would get the drug. 'We Amerindians know the forest, and use leaves and roots for medicinal purposes. This knowledge is handed down from generation to generation, this would be easy,' he assured the group.

He took the bottle the pilot had given him, and then went into the night in search of some herbs and leaves. He returned shortly after with some leaves protruding from his back pocket and a bottle of water. He rubbed the leaves in his palm and a few drops of liquid oozed from his cupped hand. He tilted the bottle and guided the liquid potion into the mouth of the bottle. He then took the bottled water laden with the poison to the grateful pilot who gulped it down and let out a satisfying burp. After a few minutes he returned and informed the group that the pilot was knocked out cold and may be sleeping for roughly half an hour.

They had to hurry before what had happened was discovered. They hastened to the plane, freed Henry and were soon retracing their steps to camp with the two packages. Henry thanked them profusely for saving his life. They hadn't gone far when they heard shouts mingled with the patter of heavy pursuing feet. With nothing to help them but the overwhelming power of the darkness and the expertise of the guide, they began a desperate race against vast odds and possible death.

The pursuing gang was using torchlights to scan the surroundings. Torchlights flickered, searching in the darkness, and it became obvious that they had no idea whether Henry had freed himself. The gang started to fire gunshots into the night sky.

It was sporadic at first but then it became more concentrated and prolonged. They were frustrated and desperate. Keith suggested that they seek cover as a bullet whistled past his left ear.

'I know of a place where we could hide,' Dukan informed them. He led them through a narrow winding trail then further up the mountain. They clawed at the sharp rocks and often slipped on the smooth wet boulders. At last they emerged on to what seemed to be a plateau. Their hands were bruised and their legs aching but the approaching voices and the incessant crack of gunfire echoing and reechoing through the maze of valleys and caves spurred them on.

They reached the edge of the plateau and under Dukan's direction joined hands and with their backs to the face of the mountain edged their way slowly and painstakingly away from the pursuers. The voices and gunfire faded away and the flashes of light became more infrequent until the mountain was again clothed in darkness and nature's quietude.

Henry was now fully recovered and in better spirits. He assured the others that he was fine and said that he was treated very well until his roommate Bollers, and Walcott, arrived and told them that he was extremely dangerous. The rescuers were now off the mountain but Dukan advised that they remain hidden until it was safe to head back to camp. They then started the long arduous trek back in the darkness of the night. The moon, sovereign of the night and her helpers, the stars, had remained cloaked. The trek back to camp took two hours and it was long after midnight when they arrived tired, battered and bruised.

Mr. Cheong told them about the attempted arson, then tucked the message into James' hand. 'It isn't relevant now, but you can have it.'

James admitted that he was too tired to do anything and wanted to get into bed. They praised and thanked Dukan and Carlos for all the help they had given them. Mr. Cheong made a mental note to report their heroism to the authorities so that they could be honoured accordingly. Dukan and Carlos departed and the boys clutched the two packages and retired to the inviting privacy of their tent.

'Wonder what are in these?' Henry said, as they tore away the brown paper wrappings from the packages.

'Jumping shrimps!' Keith exclaimed with concern. 'Do you know what this is? It's a high power telescopic rifle, capable of hitting a pin head at three hundred metres, it's used only by expert snipers and assassins.'

'So that's it, headquarters must hear about this immediately,' said James.

The other package contained a collection of fossilized rocks, a few samples of other mineral rocks, granite, manganese, a blow pipe and a feathered headdress.

James called army headquarters while Henry and Keith tried unsuccessfully to get through to police headquarters. The weather condition was poor; consistently, they failed to establish contact with either headquarters.

'By the way, there's to be another drop. Managed to pick that up when Schmidth was talking to Walcott, but I don't know when,' Henry informed them.

'Did you say Schmidth?' Keith asked.

'Schmidth,' Henry said thoughtfully.

'Wait a minute, where have I heard that name before?' he said. 'That's it, I knew it!' He suddenly exclaimed, 'Paul Schmidth! He's the American Missionary who disappeared from Morawanna Mission, after establishing a church there, everyone thought that he was dead. They even had a memorial service for him.'

'Reverend Paul Schmidth, but he was reportedly drowned. He's dead as far as the authorities are concerned,' said Keith.

'That's just what they wanted. Reverend Schmidth dies at Morawanna, then turns up alive at Dawana to master mind a massive smuggling scheme and some foreign plot to overthrow the Government. Then possibly hand over power to Walcott and a few other political fanatics. He then snatches a few millions or even billions and disappears.'

'No wonder they couldn't find him at Morawanna. He was four hundred miles away,' said Henry.

'I never trusted those Missionaries. They come out of nowhere, Bible in hand and to convince the authorities of their religiosity, establish a church, and after a few years hold the natives under their spell,' Keith added.

They again tried to establish contact with Georgetown but to no avail. They had valuable information but no means of getting it through to the authorities. They were extremely frustrated.

'If we don't get this news to Georgetown by afternoon, I'm afraid that we have to tackle this on our own,' said James.

'Well, if we have to do it on our own, it's for the good of the country. We are doing this for our country and if it comes to dying, I'll do so without fear,' said Keith.

James looked through the opening of the tent and remembered a quote from the epic poem 'Horatius,' by Lord Macaulay, 'how can a man die better than facing fearful odds for the ashes of his fathers and the temple of his gods.' It was raining and James had just realized that the tarpaulin was flapping hideously, there was a forked flash in the black sky. Lightening. He listened expectantly for the distant roll and clap of thunder, lightening's inseparable companion. He counted the seconds; four elapsed before he heard the deafening sound. Involuntarily, his hands sought the warmth of his pockets. He felt a piece of paper and pulled it out. It was the piece Mr. Cheong had given him.

'Take a look at this,' he called across the barrel that acted as a makeshift table.

In the dim glow of the paraffin lamp, Keith read the note.

WE HAVE YOUR FRIEND
WE'LL GET YOU!
TELL US WHERE TO FIND
THE WEALTH OF THE MOUNTAIN
OR NEVER SEE HIM AGAIN!

'Poor guys,' laughed Henry. 'They mean they had me.'

'Sure, what baffles me is, 'The Wealth of the Mountain,'' said James. 'I wonder if the rock paintings give the clue to the hidden storehouse or the wealth as implied by this note.'

He brought the others up to date with what Mr. Cheong had told him. Then eagerly, they settled down to figuring out and deciphering the message of the rocks. For two hours, they shifted the pieces of paper and made assumptions and diagrams of the petroglyphs, but arrived at no solution. The rain and thunder had stopped and a strong wind hurried the remnants of the dark clouds further east, leaving the sky a massy blue with the crescent moon hanging delicately over the distant trees. Henry was nodding sleepily, and so were the others. Just then an inviting wisp penetrated the under half of the canvas and extinguished the dying flame of the oil lamp. No one bothered about relighting it. They crawled sleepily into bed. It was only about two hours to day break.

TRAPPED IN A CAVE

James couldn't sleep. He thought of home and his mind raced to the tragic end of his father and the loss of his mother. Emptiness consumed him as he reminisced. He visualized his worrying colleagues he had left at the Applefarm's South Ruimveldt home. What of Eddie? He must be itching with a desire to rejoin his two pals. Suddenly, there was an urgency and determination to solve the mysteries. He eased himself on to the cold ground and felt his way across the tent, to the lamp. It was again put into operation. He picked up the pencil that lay idly where he had left it, and then laid the diagram of the petroglyphs on the top of the barrel. There were ten sketches; five made of the North Kanuku and five of the South. He couldn't help but marvel at the magnitude of the work the Guyana Archaeological Surveys had done under the directorship of Mr. Cheong.

He laid the petroglyphs of the North above the ones from the South and looked at the prominent features then at the dominant human representations, but still he made no progress. Half an hour later a fresh round of drowsiness overpowered him and he raised his arms into the air and stretched. He yawned and gulped down a mouthful of air. In that crude but relaxed posture, he bent his head to survey the sketches once again before he crawled into bed. He was confronted by an extraordinary sight, a human form in almost the exact position as he was.

'What a coincidence!' he exclaimed as his hands slid mechanically back to his sides. 'It's in the hands, it's in the hands!' Like Archimedes of ancient Greece, he had achieved his eureka moment. There was an unmistakable pattern, the hands of the

Southern region sketches pointed in the opposite direction to the other sketches from the North.

James assembled the ten sketches and numbered them. He then awoke Keith and Henry who by this time were snoring and in dreamland. He blurted out that he had deciphered the pattern in the sketches. The two sleepy eyed sleuths Keith and Henry perked up when the realization of what James had said hit them. They hurriedly took up positions around their makeshift table.

The flap of the tent shifted open to reveal a human form. They gasped in fear at the sudden intrusion but soon relaxed when they saw it was Mr. Cheong. He told them that the guards had awoken him and informed him that they had seen lights, heard talking and seen movements in the tent. He had merely come to investigate and ensure that everything was okay.

After a brief pause, James began his explanations and with the expert knowledge of Mr. Cheong the pieces were finally pieced together. 'This must be the site,' James pointed out as he ran his pencil over the sketches these five figures from the South join with the ones from the North.

'The only place they join in reality is in the Kanuku Mountains,' interjected Mr. Cheong with unbridled exuberance.

James showed them that the two adjoining arms formed what resembled a plateau with a steep wall.

'Weren't we creeping and crawling along a plateau when trying to escape from those thugs earlier?' Henry asked and the others concurred.

James then wanted to know why the sun in the sketches was directly overhead and to this, Mr. Cheong explained that to the ancient Amerindians that meant to travel due north.

They agreed that there was now something to work on, relocate the plateau then start digging north but James objected, pointing out that north could be anywhere from there to Brazil. They saw the logic of his argument and further resigned themselves to solving the mystery of the sketches.

Mr. Cheong was pensive; he paced the mud hardened floor and lit a cigar between his thumb and fore finger as he pondered the situation. He said that there was a vital element missing and that when he figured that out all the details would be revealed. A few minutes later, he blurted out that he had gotten the clue he so badly wanted. The others crowed around the dimming light as he pointed out what looked like a crude circle with an animal in the center. He explained that the symbol was for a cave entrance and gleefully announced that they may not have to dig at all.

'So, if our hunch is right,' said Keith, 'we'll be wrapping up this case before next week.'

'Yeah, we'll solve the Mystery of the Rock Painting, but, don't forget the gun drop, that is our major concern,' said James.

They retired to bed shortly after and slept soundly for an hour before they were roused by workers constantly passing their tent. They changed and hurrying outside learnt that Mr. Cheong was going to the mountains. They hurriedly prepared and within a few minutes the expedition was on its way. They all had packed breakfast comprising of tiptop cheese, bread and a water bottle of lemongrass tea.

Before 7:30 that morning, they were at the foot of Mountain Itabali in the Kanuka Range. The expedition consisted of all but two of the guards who were left at camp. Four Amerindians accompanied them and their knowledge of the mountain trail proved invaluable. The amazing thing about the journey was the way in which the non-natives carried their equipment in back packs and the natives their warishis slung across their foreheads. The plateau was one hundred-fifty meters up, but because of the steep incline and sharp jutting rocks, they did not reach it until after three hours.

When they got to the top, only the guides showed no signs of fatigue. They rested on the top of the plateau. James, Henry, Mr. Cheong and Keith sat apart from the others and looked at the sketches. 'That's the plateau we are on,' said James, 'over there is the ledge. A bit further on are the caves.'

'It's a pity we couldn't get Dukan and his son to come with us, they know this mountain well,' said Keith.

James radioed camp and reported that everything was progressing as planned. He then tried contacting army and police headquarters, but, no contact whatever could be established. He became worried. 'No contact can be made, no report can get through to Georgetown. We're in a good fix. Four days now, I haven't heard from Supt. Clarke,' he murmured.

When they were fully rested, they crossed the ledge and for the first time James saw the deep ravine that lay under. They held their breath as they edged their way over another deep narrow gorge. Reaching the other side, the guides took them down a narrow path between two over hanging ledges, then finally through a large opening in the mountain face. They now had a commanding view of both the North and South regions. A few rectangular thatched huts seemed nailed against the vast low lying Rupununi sands.

'There are the caves,' said the Amerindian guide.

Against the hard, rough face of the mountain, hundreds of small openings greeted the roving eyes. With torches, they entered the maze of winding caves. Mr. Cheong and the others searched the walls of the caves, overturned rocks and dug in a few places for peculiar signs, but, nothing was unearthed.

'There are eighteen of us, what if we form nine groups and each pair report after twenty minutes searching,' suggested Henry.

This suggestion was accepted and after sorting themselves into the groups they entered different openings in the mountain face. James and Henry formed one group, and Keith coupled with Mr. Cheong. James and Henry found themselves in a large cave with three inner compartments. They explored each one but found nothing of consequence so they retraced their steps to report to the others. Four pairs had already returned and after telling of their ill-luck they sat on rocks to await the return of the others.

It was approaching 2 p.m. and all but two pairs had returned. After waiting for a further twenty minutes and nothing was seen or heard of them, they became concerned and were organizing search parties, when they saw four figures emerge from an opening much higher up the mountain. It was the missing four. When they joined the others, they told of following their respective caves until the caves appeared ended, only to find themselves in a larger opening which seemed to be the terminating point of five or more caves. They said it looked like an ancient conference room.

'Why did you remain so long?' asked Mr. Cheong.

'We hadn't a watch to check the time,' admitted a short, squatty soldier volunteer. 'Then you see I found some queer drawings on the wall of the cave, so I stopped to make a few sketches. I love prehistoric art you know!'

Mr. Cheong requested the sketches the solider had made and to their surprise, it was identical to the sketches James had pieced together!

'We may be nearing the find, after years of research and hard work!' he exclaimed.

Before he could finish, a rifle shot was heard and he fell limply forward. Keith and Henry rushed forward to the wounded man. Blood was streaming from the side of his shoulder. The others looked in the direction of the sound only to find to their utter dismay that they were surrounded by about twenty armed men. Their hands went instinctively over their heads in surrender. Unarmed and greatly out-numbered, they surrendered meekly.

'Seems to be the gang,' said James. 'No one is to try anything heroic, dead men can't fight back,' he cautioned.

A white man emerged from the rocks carrying a rifle similar to the one Dukan had snatched for the boys.

'Don't try any dirty tricks or you will all be dead as these rocks,' he said in an unmistakable American accent.

All turned simultaneously as a groan came from the ground. It was Mr. Cheong. His eyes opened laboriously and he rose to his knees, then stood up on groggy legs. Men began rising from all around the mountain and converged on the overpowered group. It was obvious that Schmidth had an army, heavily armed and well trained and definitely well fed.

'There are Walcott and Bollers,' Henry whispered. 'The white man is the missionary Schmidth!'

Their captors numbered about one hundred and fifty and included Amerindians, Indians, Africans and the occasional 'blue eye of the European.' They were herded against a wall of the mountain by the gun wielding gang.

Schmidth laughed haughtily, 'Well, well, if it isn't my old friend Mr. Hugh Cheong.'

Mr. Cheong recognized the face of the rebel missionary, 'You are dead, you were drowned!' he exclaimed.

'Not at all my good friend. Did they find my body? I couldn't die and leave all this wealth behind, such wealth untold in these mountains! It's a pity you wouldn't be alive to tell of what you have seen,' he snarled.

'But there isn't any wealth,' said Mr. Cheong.

'I know it isn't found yet, but you'll find it for me, I've been following your progress,' he said as he clapped his hands.

Other men appeared and approached Mr. Cheong.

'These are my men! They deserted me and left for Georgetown,' he said.

'They were your men under my orders,' he boasted. 'They love money and that is what I have to give them. What were your incentives?'

Bollers walked up to Schmidth and pointed to Henry and James.

'Yes, Mr. Clarke, I've heard a lot about you. Your nose is too big, I see! Always finding it in the wrong place, but, there is no time to lose now. By tomorrow your Prime Minister and Army Commander would be dead and Major Blades would be Prime Minister with Walcott and Bollers as advisers.'

'Who'll kill them?' asked James.

Schmidth laughed, 'It's good to satisfy your curiosity before you die! They would be assassinated by the two best marksmen in the world, my trained mercenaries.'

'May I ask who are these mercenary marksmen?' asked James.

'Paul Schmidth and Denny Bollers,' he said speaking freely.

'Impossible, you alone cannot seize power,' said James.

'I do not want power, I want the wealth of the mountain; the gold of the Amerindians,' he said. 'The wealth must be mine! I only back the coup because of the security it provides me in pursuing the gold. I have the loyalty of my soldiers, and if I die, they will commit suicide rather than be caught and hanged for treason or murder.'

'You are mad Schmidth,' said Mr. Cheong.

'You'll die horribly, Paul Schmidth,' James added.

Schmidth laughed, 'I can inform you friends that at this time I am indeed dying. You begin dying the minute you are born, but in death, there is eternal peace and solace.'

'We waste too much time with them,' said Walcott. 'Remember the plane would be here tonight.'

'Stupid brat! Who are you to tell me that I waste time?' Schmidth shouted.

The captives were herded into the cave with twenty fully armed guards while Schmidth gave orders to his men. James thought of the guns at camp, but escaping seemed out of the question.

Mr. Cheong, though wounded, managed to reach the inner caves with the help of the four men who had accidentally stumbled on the rock paintings. Numerous torches and lamps brightened the surrounding walls. The captors and the captives were likewise astonished at the spectacle which met their eyes. The walls were adorned with sketches of animals, insects and human forms.

'This seemed to be the meeting place of the extinct people,' said Schmidth. 'The wealth must be around here somewhere.'

He detailed some of his men to search for the other openings, but after frantic efforts nothing was found. Schmidth became worried. It was approaching three o'clock.

'The planes are due here at six, we must find the wealth, we must!' he shouted. 'I'll kill you one by one until you find the wealth. Shoot that one,' he hissed pointing to James.

Four strong arms grabbed him and pushed him against the wall. James did not want to die, without putting up a fight. He lashed out wildly at his assailants.

'I'll shoot you myself,' said Schmidth. 'Pin him to the wall!'

'Bash his face in!' said Bollers.

'Stop, you brutes!' shouted Mr. Cheong. 'Would you spare his life if I find the wealth?'

'Yes, he'll be saved from dying now, but you'll all die when the wealth is mine!' said Schmidth tersely.

Bollers rushed over to the leader. 'Mr. Schmidth, there is a secret wall and door!' said Bollers excitedly.

Schmidth examined the door then ordered pickaxes to bash in the massive structure. The hewn rock door slowly caved in to reveal wealth untold. Schmidth rushed forward, and shouted, 'Good Lord! It's here! The wealth of the mountains! It's mine! All mine!' he said. 'Tie their hands behind their backs!' he added. His men hurried to carry out his orders.

THE GANG IS RESCUED

Schmidth ordered them into the inner room. The room proved to be a store house. Huge urns and other massive rock containers were overloaded with gold nuggets and diamonds.

'Good Christ, that stuff is worth millions of dollars!' exclaimed Mr. Cheong. 'If that mad man gets away with this, Guyana would be poor forever!'

'I'll make a break for it,' said James as he dashed for the opening.

An Amerindian guard saw his attempted escape and ended it with a crashing blow to his head. He slumped forward heavily on the rocky ground.

'That is what you'll get if you try to escape. The next man who tries would receive a bullet through his heart,' said Schmidth.

More rope was brought and their hands and feet were tightly tied together. With guards still watching them, they saw their hopes of escaping vanish.

'Only a miracle can save us now,' said Henry, who was bound to one of the guides. He turned his head slightly to the right and found himself staring at the unconscious form of James.

Schmidth gave orders and workers started to transport the gold, diamonds and other precious articles from the room in which they had laid undisturbed for centuries. Time was running out for both parties. The captors had a schedule with a plane and the captives had an appointment with death. A long line of Amerindian workers relayed the finds in lighter sacks to the outside.

'Bring the dynamite,' ordered Schmidth.

When this was done, be began setting the charges. 'For your kindness in finding the wealth for me, I'll repay you with a slow death. When all the treasure is transported outside I will press this plunger and there it is, you'll be sealed within this silent mountain,' Schmidth said to Mr. Cheong.

James' eyes flickered open. 'It's good of you to be back with us,' Schmidth laughed mockingly. 'I want to see how you will get away this time, Mr. Clarke.'

They listened in horrified silence at the tale of their ultimate doom. When Schmidth and his gang had finished extracting the wealth from the room they withdrew all the lights. It was total darkness; the room seemed as deep as space and black as eternity. There was a distant departure of feet and weird chuckles. Was it doom's dreaded signal?

'Goodbye friends, I'll say a prayer for you!' Schmidth said laughing.

This was not necessary, for each one was bidding the other farewell and asking his respective deity to accept his final prayer and soul.

Seconds later there was a deafening explosion and a rumble as rocks and boulders disturbed by the violent detonation of the dynamite, slowly rolled down the mountain face sealing off the entrance to the cave. The expedition was entombed. Salty tears rained silently on the faces of the anguished men.

'We are not dead yet,' said James. 'We are only bound and entombed.'

'The air would soon be finished and we'll all die,' said Henry.

Their spirits were low. They gave up all hope of survival so they settled down to reminiscing. Each told of his sorrows and joys. They joked and even wept.

'Wonder what the two guys we left at camp are doing?' asked Henry.

'Probably awaiting a radio report,' said James.

'If they only knew, they could get help and save us,' said Henry.

'By then, we'll be all dead either by lack of oxygen or starvation.'

They twisted and turned their hands in the darkness but the knots were expertly tied. James twisted his hands behind his back allowing Henry to look at the illuminated numerals of his watch.

'It's five-thirty. The plane would be here in another half an hour and wham! By seven, they'll be heading for Georgetown to assassinate the Prime Minister and Brigadier Gillis,' moaned James.

Mr. Cheong advised them to stop all the talking as a way to extend the use of the much needed oxygen. In total darkness and utter silence, they waited for death as patiently and quietly as the desert dweller of the Sahara waits for the seldom rain. They heard each other snores and experienced the turbulence of the flow of blood through their veins. Breathing became more laborious as the oxygen in their cell was slowly thinned. Coughing and sneezes mingled with infrequent gasps for air punctuated the silence. The end was near, crawling and clawing at them like a sloth on the underside of an enormous trunk.

Then they heard it. A sound! Was it one of the trapped men's dying call? No! It was a distinct, 'Hello.' With failing strength they responded. 'We are in here,' they chorused.

Was it death assuming a human form and playing its last trick on the minds of dying men?

'We'll get you out,' said a voice.

James thought he recognized the voice. Was it his uncle, or the deadening effects of the rocks were changing the intonation to suit its own weird cause?

Rocks were thrown aside and boulders rolled aside. Light and air rushed into the room as the cave entrance was being reopened. Nostrils and mouths opened to gulp down the intoxicating oxygen. Voices and hurrying feet were heard and torchlights approached searchingly. They were saved.

'James,' a voice called. 'Where are you, Henry are you all right?'

They were too weak to answer.

They were cut loose and taken to the plateau. There they saw for the first time their rescuers: Eddie, Supt. Clarke, a company of fully armed soldiers and the two soldiers who were left at the camp, along with Dukan and Carlos.

'We are sure glad to see you,' said Eddie. 'Seems like you two have been busy he said with a smile'

'We thought we were dead,' said Henry.

'Uncle Patrick, the gang is expecting a plane to take Schmidth and Bollers to assassinate Brigadier Gillis and Prime Minister Ross, we must stop them,' said James urgently, the mere thought revitalizing his spirits.

There was no time for explanations. They hurriedly gave to Carlos and Dukan to lead them to the gang's hideout. Twenty minutes later, they were strategically poised above the runaway. Supt. Clarke gave orders for the runaway to be surrounded and every one captured when the plane, which had not yet arrived, touched down.

The soldiers moved among the rocks like mercury in a silver plated spoon. With swiftness, precision and stealth they surrounded the runaway crouched and waited. Ten minutes later in the fading light the drone of the air craft engine was heard. Schmidth's workers ran onto the runaway and lit the boundary signals. The plane circled three times and then banked low. The landing rear was engaged and locked and the plane descended with titled wheels then taxied to a halt. It then turned gracefully like the peacock at the Botanic Gardens and rolled forward to meet the welcoming party of Schmidth, Bollers and Walcott.

The door slid back a figure in the Guyana Army uniform climbed down the rope ladder.

'My God!' exclaimed Supt. Clarke as he recognized the individual. 'That's Major Blades!'

'He's tied up with them. When the Prime Minister dies, he would become the Supreme Commander of the Armed Forces,' James said.

The Amerindian workers again began transporting packages to and from the aircraft, this time under the supervision of Major Blades, Denny Bollers, Alfie Walcott and Schmidth. At signals from Supt. Clarke and Sergeant Keith Whyte, the company of soldiers emerged from concealment and advanced slowly and deliberately in military formation towards the surprised gang. They discharged a barrage of thunderous gunfire into the air. There was no way of estimating the number of men firing and this scared the gang. Most of Schmidth men dropped their weapons and fled. They were in complete disarray and scared to death. A few Amerindians tried desperately to escape but were shot in their legs. Major Blades sensing that the game was up, pulled a revolver from his hip holster and shot wildly. Two soldiers fell forward bleeding from the arms, but the others moved forward menacingly and unrelentingly. Schmidth tried to escape, but was captured. Handcuffs were taken out by a soldier carrying a duffle bag across his shoulder. Two other soldiers stepped forward, secured their weapons and helped him put handcuffs on all the members of the gang. Other soldiers produced massive battery powered search lights that illuminated the mountain and the surrounding forests. They conducted a thorough search and rounded up the entire gang.

When Schmidth saw James and Henry, he cursed vehemently and shouted, 'I'll get even with you if it's the last day of my life.'

'That is if you leave the place where you'll be sent,' retorted Henry with a chuckle. 'To the best of my knowledge it's a long way to swim from the maximum detention center at Mazaruni.'

'Save your comments and remarks for when you are at Brickdam,' said Supt. Clarke and then turning to Major Blades with scorn and disdain he told him, 'Guyana can do well without you.'

Major Blades spat at him and continued a profanity laced tirade.

Supt. Clarke relayed a radio message to Georgetown that the mystery had been solved, the impending rebellion crushed and all the perpetrators arrested. He and the Brigadier spoke for half an hour and made decisions to have the prisoners transported to the capital. This done, they were able to settle down and reflect on all that had taken place over a matter of a few days. There was contentment and pride in each person's face for a remarkable accomplishment.

Early the following morning, seven transport helicopters landed at Mount Itabali. Among the first to disembark was Captain Persaud.

'It seems as though I've missed all the fun,' he said.

'You missed all the fun, but you've not missed the pepperpot the army boys were preparing,' joked James.

'Come on pals, you know I would have been of great help,' Eddie said.

Just then Dukan and Carlos strolled up. Eddie rushed to meet them.

'Wait a minute Eddie, do you know these two heroes?' Henry asked.

'Of course! This is my father and Carlos, my younger brother,' he shouted.

James and Henry took turns in telling Eddie the heroic roles that his father and brother had played in helping them to solve the mystery.

About nine o'clock that morning, the helicopter took the boys back to camp to collect their belongings. For their courageous work, Carlos and Dukan were given a ride with the boys in the helicopter. It was an experience they vowed never to forget, having never driven in a motorized vehicle like a car or truck before.

Carlos hinted, 'Pa, you know I want to become a pilot and fly helicopter and planes from Georgetown to Dawana and from Ogle to Lethem.'

Dukan laughed, 'I think the best thing is to wear this green uniform and with guns protect our country against men like Schmidth and Walcott.'

Later in the day, the helicopter returned to Georgetown minus twenty soldiers, who had remained to set up a temporary outpost primarily to guard Schmidth's precious den of guns and ammunition and the wealth of the mountains until they were airlifted to Georgetown.

Back in Georgetown, the prisoners were escorted to the Brickdam Police Station to await formal charges against them. A few things still baffled the boys, so they asked Supt. Clarke to fill in the gaps. Supt. Clarke told them that they had been informed about Major Blades' contacts with an American ammunition firm. When Blades heard this, he blamed Bollers for misplacing a confidential document at the college.

'So that's how we got mixed up in the affairs, Bollers thought we had sneaked the information to army headquarters,' laughed Henry.

'A pity we didn't,' said Eddie, 'but how did the petroglyphs reach the Education room?'

'Well, Walcott informed us that they had a meeting there and 'that fool Bollers' dropped it,' said Supt. Clark. 'Apparently Bollers planned to leave documents for them in the room and as a precaution tried to scare others who may be suspicious of them by triggering the shade to fall. That didn't work out so well.'

'Bollers made many mistakes, one was replacing that envelope in my room,' said James.

'He mentioned that it wasn't a mistake, and that the dormitory supervisor was the one who saw the envelope in the corridor and put it on your table,' he said.

The boys strolled with Supt. Clark as they saw the prisoners in their confines. When Blackie saw Eddie, he cursed Antonio for not shooting him but rather leaving him to hang by some weird and bizarre ritual he had seen in Southern Africa.

Supt. Clarke further explained that he and other top army personnel left the country secretly and had managed to convince the U.S. Government of the serious threat to South American security and peace efforts.

When further questioned, Bollers and Walcott admitted to having planted the bomb in the boys' car and Alfie Walcott admitted to having tried to run them down. Under intense interrogation, other names were mentioned and by afternoon, the entire gang was rounded up.

Supt. Clarke informed the boys that the Prime Minister had called an impromptu meeting at his office. They then departed Brickdam Police Station, traveling east along Brickdam and under the Independence Arch, a gift from England when Guyana attained independence from Great Britain in 1966.

The drive to the Prime Minister's office took approximately ten minutes. When they arrived an immaculately dressed soldier opened the massive gate. He stood ramrod straight, saluted smartly and waved them on. Inspector Jordan, who was driving, took a short right turn and stopped in front of a heavy sculptured wooden door guarded on either side by two soldiers in ceremonial green and white uniform and red berets. Eddie wondered what species of wood the door was made of. Was it purple heart, or some other hard wood? His thoughts drifted to the masterpiece round table displayed at the National Museum handcrafted from more than a hundred species of authentic Guyanese wood. He couldn't remember how many small pieces were used in its construction. What he could remember vividly from his school outings to the museum was the printing press used to produce the world's rarest stamp the one cent magenta printed in England in 1856 and the model of the pork knocker washing for gold nuggets on the Mazaruni.

The Prime Minister, who apparently was always briefed and kept informed by his top officers, profusely thanked the boys for the vital role they had played in bringing the mystery to a successful conclusion and suggested that a special function be held to honour all those who had participated in the various operations. He even mentioned that Dukan, Carlos and some other native patriots be brought to Georgetown for the ceremony. Eddie wondered if the venue would be the National Culture Center, the Umana Yama, the lawns of the Prime Minister's Residence or the Pegasus Hotel. He smiled and said in soliloquy, 'Wherever it is, Anita and Mrs. Applefarm will never forget the experience and neither will my father and brother.'

When the meeting with the Prime Minister ended, the boys departed for army headquarters where the gang was being under constant armed guard. They thanked Brigadier Gillis for his help, gave him an awkward civilian salute and headed for his uncle's home in Prashad Nagar. When they got there, the old watchman opened the gate and commented that he hadn't seen the boys for some days. 'We were out of town,' James informed him as he parked the car.

'So was your uncle, he called one evening to say that he was okay and not to worry about his absence,' he said.

'That's just like him,' said James.

The watchmen then asked them if they had heard anything about a gang of men who had plans to overthrow the government.

Henry was about to answer when James asked the watchmen who his source of information was. He said that for the last hour there were news flashes. James advised him to continue monitoring the news broadcasts and told James and Eddie that they had better contact the girls immediately. They excused themselves and hurried inside.

James dialed Anita. The phone rang once and Mrs. Applefarm answered as though she was waiting for the call. 'Is it James?' she asked.

'Yes, it is,' he answered.

Mrs. Applefarm broke into tears. 'James, I was hoping that one of you would have telephoned. It's dreadful,' she said between sobs.

'What's the matter, Mrs. Applefarm?' he asked between her crying. He had to be very patient and understanding knowing her frailty.

'Anita, Shelly and Abiola are all sick in bed some kind of unknown ailment,' she told him.

'Have you taken them to the doctor?' he inquired.

'Yes, that's the first thing I did,' she said. 'About three days ago they went shopping for craft work by the Vreeden Hoop Stelling behind the fire station. They saw a toy canoe being sold by a Bibi Mohammed of Warapana Pomeroon and decided to buy it. Since then, they have been receiving offers to resell it at unbelievable prices. The offers have now become threats. We are all afraid James,' she said.

'Mrs. Applefarm, we will be coming over immediately,' James reassured her.

James told Henry and Eddie about the girls' ailment and advised that they go to the Applefarm's right away. They changed their clothes, jumped into James' car and headed to Mrs. Applefarm's home to see the girls. James, Henry and Eddie were not aware that they were heading into a more intriguing mystery 'The MYSTERY OF THE GOLDEN CANOE.'

ABOUT THE AUTHOR

Claurence D. C. Johnson is a former teacher. He holds a trained teacher's certificate and a bachelor's of science degree in political science. He has taught in Guyana, St. Lucia and the Bahamas. He and his children currently reside in America.